AFFINITY
AN ANTHOLOGY

Winston Salem, North Carolina

This book is a work of fiction. Names, characters, places and incidents either are products of the authors' imagination or are used fictitiously. Any resemblance to actual events or locales or persons living or dead is entirely coincidental.

Digestivo, Sand Castles, Couples Project and *Interstate Exit* by Jim Doering are excerpts from *The Spaces Between*, a short story collection soon to be published by 67 Press.

Miriam's Song by Larry Lefkowitz was previously published by Wily Writers in 2010.

Cover Design by Matt Ankerson.

ISBN: 978-0-9966616-0-7

Manufactured in the United States

TABLE OF CONTENTS

AFFINITY, V
   AN INTRODUCTION

DIGESTIVO, 1
   JIM DOERING

ALL I WANT, 5
   RICHARD CABUT

A BEAUTIFUL NOISE, 12
   VICTORIA BRIGGS

COUPLES PROJECT, 24
   JIM DOERING

TOURISTS, 27
   JEFFREY GARVER

SAND CASTLES, 43
   JIM DOERING

MIRIAM'S SONG, 50
   LARRY LEFKOWITZ

WATCHING THE HOMELESS, 59
   ALAN WRIGHT

UGLY AS SIN, 66
   JEFFREY SYKES

SEXTING IS SUCH A BAD HABIT, 74
   NIKITA HERNANDEZ

TAX FREE WEEKEND FUCK FEST, 81
   DONALD GEORGE LOSEY

THE NEXT EXIT, 83
   EMILY AUMAN

VANILLA TUNA, 86
   LISA MUIR

WE END UP HERE, 97
   CHLOE JOHNSON

ROAD RASH, 104
   BRIAN CULP

DEATHWISH ON ACID, 111
   JEFFREY SYKES

INTERSTATE EXIT, 120
   JIM DOERING

ABOUT THE AUTHORS, 125

ABOUT 67 PRESS, 127

AFFINITY
AN INTRODUCTION

It's my pleasure to introduce our latest collection, Affinity: an Anthology.

As with The Salmagundi, we made no requirements for theme or content. Unlike the Salmagundi, a theme quickly emerged from the stories we began to receive. We wondered if there was something about 2014 that inspired such particular strife, but the more we thought about it and the more we read, we realized we were witness to the basic building blocks of the human condition.

Affinity has many definitions, its most common usage is "a spontaneous or natural liking or sympathy for someone or something." It's describing our attraction, be it to an object or person. The very basis of how we start our relationships. I like that, but it doesn't tell the whole story, not of our relationships, or the word itself. It's a start, it's just not complete.

The chemist, Joseph Mellor, described chemical affinity as "the driving force of a chemical reaction." Now we're getting somewhere. The Driving Force. I believe this is what we talk about when we talk about love. It's what pulls us together and allows us to react with another person. It's the reaction we tend to focus on, but it's the affinity that got us there in the first place and it's what brings us back–for good, bad or ugly.

The 17 stories you hold in your hands explore the nature of our driving forces. The results are sometimes explosive, sometimes magical and always intense. And like any memorable relationship, these stories will leave a mark. But don't let that hold you back, it's those marks that define us.

Alan Wright
67 Press
July, 2015

AFFINITY

DIGESTIVO
JIM DOERING

The couple walked into the small neighborhood bar unobserved. In the corner, a musician played love songs on a beat-up baby grand piano intended for a generation that had long ago abandoned romance. The man nodded and let the woman choose where they would sit. She gazed at the half-empty, wooden bar-top and two empty tables nearby before choosing high-backed chairs at the end. The man caught the eye of a disinterested barkeep who nodded his assent while he poured a beer for another customer.

"We've been here before," she said.

"Now that you mention it, I do remember that," he said. "We had a meal right over there." He pointed to a small alcove on the other side of the bar.

"It was a long time ago. Almost as long ago as my marriage."

"It has been awhile," he agreed, his voice a little hoarse.

The barkeep made his way over and the man asked if they stocked a certain kind of liquor, one that would be the perfect way to end their evening. "Here," he said, removing a bottle from the high shelf and setting it down on the bar top. "It's the only one we carry."

"I think that will work," the man said, staring at an unopened bottle of Armagnac.

"The glasses need to be warmed," the woman told the bartender. He hesitated a moment before giving her an almost imperceptible nod and walking to the sink at the far end of the bar. He held small brandy glasses under a stream of water for a couple of minutes until the water turned hot. Drying them, he opened the new bottle and delivered a long pour into the warmed glasses. The man and woman locked eyes and smiled at one another before grasping their drinks and touching them together softly. They inhaled the essence of the liquor and tentatively sipped.

"The perfect digestivo," she said, using the Italian word.

"It's very nice," the man replied.

"You know, in all the time we've known each other, we've never really had a fight," she said, cupping her glass in two hands to keep it warm. The musician began singing a fifty-year-old love ballad mostly in key. They both stopped at the intrusion.

"We could start a fight now, if you'd like," he said. She smiled in response and gently pressed her hand to the top of his before taking another sip. "When we were here before, we shared a bowl of mussels. Do you remember? It was a very good night."

"Like always," she said.

"And then you went home to him."

"Maybe we've never fought because we've never had time to waste," she said, changing the subject back.

"Sometimes a relationship just works," he said, glancing over at the musician, who had started another slow song. The bartender came over and asked if they needed anything. "We used to come here when this was another place," the man said, mentioning the restaurant's old name.

"Ah, that was a long time ago," the bartender replied. "I've been here eight years, and that was a few years before my time."

The man swallowed the last of his drink, and the woman poured half of what remained of hers into his glass. They slung back the remains, paid the tab, and walked out into the gentle spring night.

"This has been such a wonderful evening," she said as they walked down the street.

"The night air is glorious. I can breathe better and my throat doesn't hurt anymore."

"Your voice sounds low and sexy tonight," she said, snaking her arm through his. They walked the rest of the way down the uneven sidewalk in silence.

At his car he opened the front passenger door of the sedan for her to get in before starting it up. He drove slowly and deliberately the entire way. Arriving at her apartment building he said, "I'd get out and hug you, but I think I'm coming down with something." She opened her door, hopped out and bent down so she could see his face through the open window.

"When you're feeling well, Caro Mio, I'll give you such a big hug."

"When I'm better," he said in a raspy voice, "I'll make you forget all about hugs."

ALL I WANT
RICHARD CABUT

What you want and what you get. They're like night and day. Chalk and cheese. The Louis V bags down Deptford market and those in the actual shop. They're not the same thing at all. Not that I ever want or ask for much. Take my last birthday. Smellies? The Downton box set? The Louis V? I would have settled for a hug. I'm a cheap date! Course, I wouldn't have said no to some chocs—Surprises are good, although I was about to have a few of those soon enough that day.

I woke up and, like I said, I really fancied a cuddle. That's not a figure of speech either. There's nothing better than a good old-fashioned cosy-up. It warms the cockles of your heart and makes your toes curl all at the same time. If you could bottle the feeling, you could put the breweries and dealers out of business. But the bloke I woke up next to was having none of it. He grunted when I tried to put my arm around him: 'Geroffwillya.' He mumbled that his head hurt. Mine ached, too. My brain felt like two hoodies had been having a big, vicious dust-up in it. Slugging it out all around my bonce. Shouldn't have had those last few pints. I never learn! I was about to tell the bloke that having a hug cures all, even the blue can flu. But just then he turned around to reveal the biggest black eye ever. Not even a hug would've cured that! It was enormous—I could almost feel it throbbing...

Shut up! I'm talking about the black eye!

After seeing the shiner, I couldn't stop myself: I pointed to it and had a laugh. Very rude of me I know. The bloke seemed a bit put out at first. He touched his eye and winced. That black eye must've hurt a bit, I tell you. That'll teach him to get into scraps! Then he looked at me. I was still laughing my tits off. He gave me a big look. A puzzled look. Quizzical. He was peering at *my* face. I stopped laughing. '*What*?' I asked. Then—you know what?—*he* started laughing. In fact, he was having a right noisy giggle. You know that saying 'he who laughs last...'? Well, the bloke seemed like he was definitely having the final chortle. He was laughing so hard that, for a minute, I thought the acne on his chest would erupt. I looked at him blankly, mouth open. I raised an eyebrow in an inquiring sort of way. The bloke pointed at me. 'Take a look in the mirror, darling,' he said in between sniggers. I thought to myself: what *is* he on about? Have I got a spot on my nose? So what if I have. Big deal! I can go into the bathroom and have a squeeze. A good, satisfying pop. In fact, I thought, sod the bathroom, right here and now in bed will do. I know it's the first date... if you can call it that. And it's a well-known fact that you should never squeeze anything but your bloke's hand, or whatever, on a first date. But, let's be honest: there isn't going to be a second date. There never is. So, sod it, I went to grab a mirror from the bedside cupboard. I dug through all the crap I'd dumped in there. Empty crisp packets and, what's this? Half a biccy! Ooh, good find. I'll have that later, I thought. But where's the mirror? I can never find anything I need when I want it. Oh, here it is under a few scrunched up tissues. Yuk. So, anyway, I held the mirror up to my face. Sucked in my cheeks. Pouted my lips. Gave it the rock star stare from all angles.

What did I see? Nothing. Except the usual nasty wear and tear—enough of it to wring a little teardrop out of the corner of a girl's bloodshot eye. If I'd let it. But I didn't and I don't. I make sure my waterworks stay turned off. Never show 'em you're hurting. Never show 'em you're feeling every pinch and poke that it—life in all its gory glory that is—gives you. Never.

And then I opened my mouth to speak. I was going to tell the bloke: 'Nothing here to laugh at, so button it!' And that's when I noticed something weird in the mirror. I opened my mouth a little more and looked closely.

Arggh!

I had another big look.

Arggh!!!

My hangovers are bad, but I never hallucinate. Well, hardly ever. No, this was real... in fact, like they say, here was 'too *much* reality'.

Where my two front teeth, my big pearly whites, should have been was... nothing! A void. A black hole. Mind the sodding gap!

Somehow, between leaving the pub and crashing out cold with the bloke, my front teeth had been knocked out!

How? No flaming idea! I must've been well numbed by the booze, 'cause my mouth didn't hurt more than usual, and I hadn't a clue that the choppers had actually gone till I looked. I had another sneaky peak in the mirror. Squinting in the hope that if I took a cheeky sideways glance, it would be all right somehow. Like they say, it'll be all right on the night. But this was the morning and it wasn't all right. It never is.

In the mirror, I looked like the back of a bus. In fact, I looked like I'd been thrown off the back of a bus. Which, come to think of it, might just have been how I'd lost my teeth! I use the word 'think' loosely 'cause, really, it was like the cogs in my head were rusty and clogged. The sound they made was like some horrible grating, 'Krrrrrr-rrrraghfffffkkgggg!' in my brain.

I just wanted a hug! But the bloke was edging away from me and, in any case, this was no time to cry over spilt milk. Or, even over spilt milk teeth. The big trouble that particular day was the eldest's grandparents, on the father's side, were due round anytime to take her out for the day. If they saw me without my biters, they'd ask all sorts of embarrassing questions. And I didn't have any answers. They might even throw their hands up in an 'oh-God-we-give-up-style' and leave without the eldest. That would be my day screwed. Besides, the eldest needed a break, too. No one ever took her out, least of all her dad.

He, the ex, was around at first, but not for long. I didn't see him for ages and then he came over on the wrong night. He said: 'I'll see the kid when I want.' I said: 'Oh, yeah?' He said: 'Yeah! You can't effing stop me seeing her whenever I want.' I said: 'You think?' He said: 'If I want to effing see her tonight I'll effing come round tonight.' I said: 'Well, you was supposed to come round last night. If you come round when you're meant to… if you do things when you're supposed to… if you do things… if you …' I stopped.

I suppose it sounded like an enigmatic silence, but the truth is sometimes I can't think of the snappy, clever thing to say. Like the time I was in the shop buying munchies and her down the road came in. 'Hob Nobs?' she said to me in the queue, in that snide tone. Meaning, are you *sure*, fatty? Looking back, I should've come up with a quick, smart reply like: 'Yeah. I like 'em. And I've heard you like Nobs, too.' But all I could do at the time was smile and nod like an idiot. I take the biscuit all right.

My ex didn't say anything either. So, finally, I said to him: 'She's okay now. She don't know any different. She's a kid. But when she gets older …' He cut me off. He was angry. He snarled. He opened his mouth. A big open black hole. A void. He shouted: 'Yeah? Well I'm effing off.' And he did.

I shook and lit a fag—just like after we, me and the ex, did it that effing night and made the eldest.

Ah, bollocks. The tongue, like they say—they say a lot of things, don't they?—is always probing the aching tooth. Not that I had many teeth left for my tongue to probe! But you know what I mean: we pick and poke at our troubles and mistakes. But there's no point in moaning on about it. There's no relief in prodding or poking at things. Anyway, I've got no regrets. I love the eldest to bits. When she was younger, there was nothing so lovely as *her* toothless grin. Not like mine, eh? Although, I've got my new snappers in right now, so you can't tell. See?

That's right! Go on! Have a laugh. Just like the bloke was doing that morning, even as he was legging it out of the door, one trouser leg on and one off. He tripped over while scrambling to get out—what a farce!—before the grandparents could show up. Blokes are like that, one mention of meeting the family and they're off as quick as a London girl's knickers. I was in a bother, though. In trouble. What could I possibly say to the grandparents! 'What's happened to my teeth? Oh, I had them out. Fashion. Keep up. No one has front teeth anymore!' Or, 'Teeth? Lost 'em getting the cap off a bottle—just goes to show: always have an opener handy!' Just then the doorbell went. Ding dong. I had to think fast.

I looked around. I was in a proper state. I scratched my head. I scratched my arse.

The bell went again, accompanied by a bit of knocking. 'You in there, girl?' said a voice through the letterbox.

'Coming!' I shouted back. I had to think very fast.

I answered the door to the old folks. Just a tiny bit at first. I peeked through the crack. 'Well, you going to let us in, girl?' they said. There was no getting out of it. I opened the door wide. They looked at me. In fact, they stared.

'What's that, girl!' they asked. I had a big scarf covering my mouth. 'I've got a cold,' I said, muffled. I laid it on thick: 'I'b god a bold'. I told them I didn't want anyone to catch it. 'The bold that I god.'

'Very thoughtful, darling. Very caring,' they said. I laughed, cause it came into my head at that moment that I was... lying through my teeth!

They took the eldest off for the day and I went back to bed. Fell in the pit. I was just drifting off, but there's no rest for the wicked 'cause just then the youngest woke me up. He got into bed, and I gave him a good cuddle. A lovely clinch. So I suppose you could say that I got my hug after all.

He's a poor little bleeder, the youngest—he should've been at school, but they won't have him. He broke someone's nose, the teachers said. Well, at least he didn't knock the kid's teeth out!

I gave him another big hug. You know what? That's what the school should do. All they've got to do is put their arms around him. Just hold him for a bit, and he's all right. Just hold him. He'll soon feel better.

People just need someone to put their arms around them...

... that's all people need...

... that and their two front bleeding teeth!

A BEAUTIFUL NOISE
VICTORIA BRIGGS

The queue for the bus stretched the length of the airport, backing all the way up to the aquarium in the arrivals hall.

'Unegrève,' said the gendarme at border control when Harry asked about the line of people visible through the other side of the glass partition.

'What strike? Why?' asked Harry, checking his phone for texts that might have come through during the flight. He'd just got off the plane from Heathrow; no-one had said anything about a taxi drivers' strike in Nice.

The gendarme shrugged and handed Harry his passport back. He waved the next person forward with two fingers, leaving Harry to shuffle to the side, still checking his phone.

There was a bus into Cannes every thirty minutes, the woman at the information desk told him. Helicopters were more frequent, but the price of a flight would have cleared him out of expenses for the week. Harry watched the record label bosses and A&R execs—the top ears of the industry—heading off towards the helipad. Even after they'd disappeared from view, you could still hear their guffaws.

The bus queue looked to be at least a couple hours long. Harry felt a burning in his stomach and started digging in his pocket for an antacid tablet.

There was a tap on his shoulder: 'Excuse me, Sir?'

A young woman, almond-eyed, was holding a piece of paper out for him to read. She was dressed in black with her head shorn at one side. There was a small tattoo of a diamond behind her left ear.

'This is bus for Cannes?' she asked.

Harry smiled and took the paper from her, holding it at arm's length.

He took his reading glasses out from his top pocket. 'This is where you're going?' he asked, pointing to the address on her hotel reservation.

'Yes. For music show.'

'I'm heading there too,' Harry looked again at the reservation, 'Sachiko?'

Sachiko laughed. 'And you?'

Harry introduced himself. 'This bus will take us to Cannes, but we have a wait I'm afraid. I hope you're not in a hurry?'

'No hurry. Music show tomorrow tonight. Warhead—you know?'

Warhead? Harry had been reading the week's itinerary on the flight over. His was the publishing side of the industry; he'd been coming to the music trade show at Cannes for the last twenty years. A professional middle-man, he licensed other people's tracks for use in games, TV ads, mobile phone ringtones—whatever paid. These days the show was as much about technology as it was about the music. The Japanese—if his memory recalled correctly–were sponsoring this year's international showcase. Warhead was one of the headliners.

'Warhead,' Harry smiled. 'The grindcore act?'

'Cool, grindcore!' said Sachiko and held her hand up for a high five. Harry obliged, assuming he'd said the right thing.

By the time they were at the front of the queue, Harry knew a lot about Warhead. Sachiko was their promoter. The band was flying in from Tokyo the next day to perform their set before starting out on a promo tour round Europe.

'France, Germany, UK. First time ever,' said Sachiko, beaming.

Heading up the Japanese trade mission was a Mr. Oshiro. He would be accompanying Warhead, and all the other acts, on their flight over tomorrow.

'Government guy,' she told him. 'Big, big honour.'

Harry sat next to Sachiko on the coach, who spent most of the journey taking photos through the window. When she'd exhausted the view, she took some of Harry, and then one of them together with both their hands locked in the sign of the horns. After she'd taken a photo, she'd text it to the band. When she wasn't sending texts, she was reading the ones buzzing back.

'Aki says it sucks so bad they come tomorrow, not today.'

'Well, tomorrow's the big day tell him.'

'Yosuke asks who you are. I tell him you're producer, right?'

'Right,' said Harry, though she wasn't even close.

Forty minutes later the coach pulled in to the south side of the town, at the far end of the Croisette, just past the marina where all the super yachts were moored. Harry walked with Sachiko as far as her hotel.

'You stay here too?'

'Oh, I'm just around the corner,' he said, waving his hand in an over-there gesture.

'Harry, you promise you come to showcase tomorrow night? Meet the guys, party?'

Harry smiled at her pronunciation of party, how it borrowed the American 't'. He gave her his business card. 'I'll be sure to look in.'

Sachiko said she was off to shower and unpack before heading out 'to network and sort shit out.' They high fived again and he watched her disappear up the hotel's driveway, towards its art deco façade, where a doorman in coat tails stepped out to greet her.

.   .   .

Harry was staying at a place opposite the train station. It had one working lift and an old girl on reception. He spent a couple hours in his room, answering emails and putting the finishing touches to a presentation he needed for the next day, before deciding to head out again for a five star nightcap.

It was a short walk back down to the beach front hotels. He'd only just arrived when he clocked Carl Peterson wandering around reception. Harry put his head down and made a bee-line for the bar, only stopping when he heard Carl shout his name above the hubbub.

'Carl,' he said. 'Just got here?'

'No thanks to the taxi drivers. Bummed a lift with Jenny Reynolds in the end. She hired a car, but then we hit a diesel spill near Antibes. Went for a skid down the motorway doing over sixty. It's lucky we got here at all.'

'Jesus. Sounds like you need a drink?'

Carl smiled. He was like a truffle pig when it came to sniffing out expense accounts. Snout in the dirt, he rummaged for favours, for the tail-end of a drinks round, for a line of toot—whatever was on offer. He put his arm around Harry's shoulders. 'Mate,' he said. 'I always need a drink.'

Harry took a seat at the bar and waited to be served. It made the ideal vantage point. From here, he watched the waiters dancing in between leather armchairs with trays balanced on fingertips, and faces looming in and out of view from behind the marble colonnades. He played with a beer mat and scanned the crowd. There was no sign of Sachiko.

'Look who I found,' said Carl, back from the bathroom.

'Jenny, good to see you,' said Harry, kissing her cheek.

'You heard about our road trip then?'

'The diesel spill? Carl told me.'

She laughed and held her hands out in front of her. 'Look at me! I'm still shaking.'

Carl snorted. 'So what? Mine do that every morning.'

'Ignore him,' said Harry. 'He's just pissed off he couldn't afford to get a helicopter ride in with the big boys.'

'Oh, and I suppose you're coining it in, Harold? That would make you one of the few left these days who is.' Carl slid his empty glass across the bar towards Harry. 'You can make mine another double in that case.'

Harry glanced around the room again, trying to spot Sachiko, but she was nowhere to be seen. There were other absences, too. A decade of downloads and streaming had killed off most of the old faces. Once of a day, this bar would have been heaving with bodies, spilling out into reception and all shouting to be heard. Now, he could count the people he recognised in single figures. It wasn't Carl's fault he just happened to be one of them. It meant while ever this merry-go-round still turned, the two of them were bound together.

Harry brandished a fifty Euro note in the direction of a waiter. 'Monsieur, I'll have another double for my friend here.'

.　　.　　.

Next morning, Harry got up early and called his ex-wife. He spoke to his youngest daughter, to wish her good luck in her exam that day, then he set off in search of something greasy.

The conference registration desk didn't open until 10. Along the Croisette, street cleaners in overalls were power-washing the pavement clear of dog shit outside the high-end boutiques. Harry walked in the road to avoid their jet sprays and the morning parade of miniature pooches. He found a free table in a café opposite some open ground, where old men in berets still played boules and smoked unfiltered cigarettes.

After breakfast, he set off for his meetings. By lunchtime he'd agreed a distribution deal in Lithuania. By mid-afternoon he was half way to signing a new sync deal on some long forgotten Balearic track.

The Japanese showcase wasn't due to start till nine that evening. Back at his hotel, Harry showered and changed. He looked at himself in the mirror: could he really still pass for a record producer?

He raked back his hair with his fingers and swapped his brogues for some new shoes he'd bought on impulse at the airport.

Jenny was already there when he arrived. He spotted her coppery hair glowing beneath a spotlight. There was another woman next to her who Harry didn't recognise. The two of them were laughing with the bartender. Flirting, he thought.

'Good day?' Jenny asked when she saw Harry.

'Not bad. Got lucky. Made a few quid.' He said, digging into a bowl of peanuts on the bar. It occurred to him that he hadn't eaten anything since breakfast. 'How about you?'

'Better than yesterday. No diesel spills at least. Think I might have drummed up some interest in the new girl I just signed.'

'Cheers to that,' said Harry and clinked his glass against hers.

'So what's happening tonight then? Can't say I've heard of any of the acts. Worth sticking around for do you reckon?'

'I hear good things about Warhead.'

'Warhead?' Jenny flicked through the write-up in the showcase guide. 'Since when was heavy your thing?

Harry shrugged. 'Since yesterday.'

A crackle from the speaker signalled the introduction to the night's events and stopped him from elaborating further.

The first act was some bubble-gum pop duo who sang their entire set in English.

Next up was a rockabilly band, a five piece in sharp suits and shiny black quiffs. Jenny took hold of his arm and started to bop to the music.

'Come on,' she said, but he shook his head. Jenny rolled her eyes and grabbed the woman she'd been talking to at the bar, the two of them working themselves up into some complicated jive routine.

Harry was content to leave them to it. His new shoes had started to pinch, and besides, he wanted to watch the showcase. It was the sponsoring nation's opportunity to generate interest in its repertoire across other markets—or at least that was how the sales guys sold it.

The showcases usually followed a standard format: different genres, a couple of commercial acts, one or two more critical contenders. Harry couldn't decide if it was genius or sheer lunacy to stick some grindcore into the programme.

He scanned the room. There was still no sign of Sachiko. Warhead was the last act. There were two more acts before their set began. Harry leant against the bar, trying to take the weight off his heels where the shoes were biting. He spotted Carl across the room, back-slapping one of the guys from the majors and braying loudly.

'Look at him,' said Jenny, her cheeks flushed from jiving. 'Saw him in the conference centre earlier—totally blanked me. Didn't even offer to pick up half the hire car cost from yesterday. Nothing.'

Harry shook his head. 'Same old Carl.'

Just as Warhead was announced, the dry ice machine started to spew and Harry glimpsed Sachiko. She was with an older man. He was shorter than her and wearing a suit. Mr Oshiro, Harry presumed. Then the lights dimmed and she was swallowed by the dark. Somebody in the crowd whistled and the band stepped out.

Harry felt a surge of acid reflux and then it began–a discordant, brutal noise assault. Guitars screamed, feedback bled from the speakers; the bass, over-amplified, hammered through him like a heart attack. The singer roared in Japanese; he growled, the microphone pressed into his mouth like a sex-gag. He stood on the edge of the stage, whipping his waist-length hair around in the twisting column of smoke. Harry watched transfixed, reminded somehow of carrion crows and wild-eyed stallions with glossy, jet manes.

Jenny dug him in the ribs. She put her mouth to his ear to say something, but he couldn't hear. She pointed to the door and gestured for him to follow, but he felt rooted to the spot. 'Sorry', he mouthed.

In the middle of the mosh pit, Harry could see Carl, flailing around like an idiot. He imagined Sachiko in their too somewhere, her slim limbs covered in a film of glistening sweat.

The set was mercifully brief. Three short songs like rapid fire–bang, bang, bang–and then it was over. The singer left the stage, knocking the microphone stand to the floor, the sound of the crash ricocheting off the walls. Harry felt in his pocket for an antacid. There was one left in the pack.

He found Jenny in the downstairs bar afterwards. 'That actually hurt,' she laughed, covering her ears with her hands. 'What are you having?'

He settled on a beer, not sure his stomach could be trusted with anything stronger.

While Jenny got the order in, he popped across the lobby to the gents, planning to swing by the concierge on the way back in search of something for his blisters.

The Japanese crowd were standing in a group together just outside the main bar. A couple of A&Rs were buzzing around the edges. Harry spotted Warhead in a corner, away from the main group. The one Harry recognised as the singer, appeared to be remonstrating with Mr Oshiro, who had his arms folded high across his chest.

'Everything ok?' said Harry, after Mr Oshiro had walked off in one direction, and the band in another.

'Harry,' said Sachiko. 'Did you see the show?'

'I did, just now. I saw it. I mean, I heard it. Wow! I can still hear it.'

Sachiko frowned. 'Mr Oshiro very angry with the guys. Said the set too short, too loud for industry crowd. Not good first impression.'

'Really?'

'He's business man. Come over to make trade deals with Europe. Not really music fan.'

'Maybe he'll find they're an acquired taste, 'offered Harry. 'Mr Oshiro might get to like them eventually. When the business deals start rolling in, at any rate.'

'The guys not really interested in business deals. Want to just play grindcore, keep pure.'

Harry could just about remember pure. He remembered it lying somewhere between boy and man, in a place far away where it was always summer. He suddenly felt gripped by a need to tell her about those days, about himself, and the way things used to be. He wanted to lean his head close to hers, to kiss the diamond tattoo behind her ear and tell her how he hadn't stopped thinking about her since the bus ride.

Sachiko was looking at the phone in her hand. It had started buzzing with texts. 'Ok, it was nice to meet you, Harry,' she said. 'I'm glad you enjoyed the show. Maybe we see you on tour some time.'

'You're leaving already?'

'Early start tomorrow. Guys want to rehearse new set before show in Paris. Gonna be so cool, right?'

Harry felt pure slipping from his memory. 'Yes, it is,' he said. 'It will be.'

She held up her hand for a high five, and he leant forward and kissed her lightly on the cheek. 'Good luck,' he told her as she left.

Across the hotel lobby, opposite the main bar, was a smaller piano bar where the lighting was dim. Harry happened to glance in as he passed. Mr Oshiro was sitting alone at one of the tables, nursing a brandy glass and watching the piano player work the ivories.

'Excuse me,' said Harry, hovering over his table. 'I apologise for interrupting your evening, only I saw you earlier at the showcase and just wanted to pass on my congratulations for that terrific last act. What an incredible performance. You must be very pleased with how it went?'

Mr Oshiro looked at him over the top of his glasses. For a second, Harry thought he wasn't going to reply. 'Warhead?' he said at last.

'That's right, Warhead. An inspired choice. The place is just buzzing with talk about them. I predict great things for them, Mr Oshiro. Great things.'

Mr Oshiro's mouth fell open a little. 'Not too much noise?' He asked.

'Mr Oshiro,' said Harry, and pressed his hands together. 'It was a beautiful noise.'

Mr Oshiro stood up and bowed deeply across the table. Harry found himself reciprocating the gesture, the piano player looking on.

Jenny was still in the main bar. 'You took your time,' she said. 'I thought you'd stood me up.'

'Sorry, bumped into a friend. Fancy a bite to eat?' He asked her. 'Only not here. Let's walk over to the old town.'

'I thought your feet were killing you?'

'They are,' said Harry and offered her his arm. 'May I?'

Jenny climbed off the bar stool and linked her arm through his. 'We're getting too old for this game,' she said.

'Don't remind me,' said Harry, limping through the lobby towards the door. The sound of the band still ringing in his ears.

COUPLES PROJECT
JIM DOERING

Charles looked at the display of his phone as it chimed, sitting on his meticulously organized workbench. He held a single horse hair paintbrush filled with black paint in one hand and a partially painted figure in the other. It was Meredith. His nose scrunched in disgust. His wife had the curious knack of always calling at the perfectly wrong moment, exactly when it was least convenient for him. He carefully placed the brush on the rim of the paint bottle and placed the British soldier from the Revolutionary War era near its perfectly painted squad mates.

"Hello."

"Charles, I'm having lunch with my friend Ellen. Could you do us a favor?" Without waiting for an answer she went on, her voice syrupy sweet, in tones and pace and words she only used when she wasn't around him. "You're so good at picking wines, I thought I might read you the new list at Claudia Bistro and you could tell us which was best."

Claudia Bistro. She knew that was one of his favorite places. He sensed the bile rise, felt throbbing at his temples. *So, I'm not good enough to dine with at one of my favorite restaurants, but I'm good enough to be your private sommelier?*

"Go on," he said, his voice thin with tension.

.   .   .

When Meredith returned home, Charles was in the kitchen filling a glass with filtered water and smiling to himself. He had finally finished the British foot soldiers. Tomorrow, they'd be dry enough to place on his ornate battlefield in the basement. Six months of work. Now he could move on to his next project.

"So what are you so happy about?" Meredith asked. "Did you get anything productive accomplished while I was gone?" Meredith set her car keys on the kitchen table and placed her purse on the seat of Charles' favorite chair.

"Oh, a couple of things," he said.

"Like what? Playing with your little toys again?"

Charles breathed deeply. "As I've told you before, *dear,* they're scaled historical miniatures. They're not *toys.*" A vein in his forehead pulsed. Meredith raised an eyebrow.

"You look a little flushed, Charles. You could use some fresh air and exercise. I worry about you stuck in that dank basement all the time. Neither of us is getting any younger. I read an article in *Cosmo* recently. It said that couples that share activities together have better relationships and even better health. I bought some annuals on my way home from Home Depot. Will you help me plant them before dinner?" Charles thought she seemed just a bit too pleased with herself.

"If I must."

"Good," she said, grasping his bicep. "I'm guessing it will only take a couple of hours. Don't forget to take an antihistamine. Now why don't you run along upstairs and change?" She grinned broadly, like a cat that had finally cornered an elusive mouse.

"Speaking of doing things together, I pulled a couple of steaks out of the freezer. I thought I'd cook dinner tonight," he said.

"What a pleasant surprise, you cooking. What's the occasion?"

"No occasion, it's just my way of contributing more around here. You know, it *is* something you've harped on me about."

"Thank you for remembering. That sounds wonderful. Now, get out of those clothes and into something more comfortable. Time's a wasting." Meredith opened the door to the garage shaking her head in surprise.

Charles whistled as he trod up the stairs. He felt a weight had been lifted. He slipped on some old cargo shorts, silently rejoicing in thoughts of finishing his battlefield. Three-hundred seventy-three individual pieces. It would take hours to parse out exactly where every soldier should be optimally placed for the best strategic and visual impact, but the effort would be more than worth it. In the meantime, he could get a jump on his next project.

It had taken less than hour to grind the castor beans into a fine powder before Meredith got home. He figured five or six doses placed strategically in her meals over the next week would do the trick. Maybe she was right. It might be nice to do more things together.

TOURISTS
JEFFREY GARVER

"Yeah, it was weird mom. It was just like: there's the British dude from *The Nanny* in an episode of *Mad Men*," Harris said to his mom on a Friday night in August from his South Carolina apartment.

"You know I always liked Fran Drescher. Maybe I should watch *Mad Men*," Mrs. Maynard responded.

"She's not in the show, mom. It's just the British father."

"I know. I'm just saying that I like Fran Drescher."

"I do too, Mom. You know, eh, I've got to go. I've got some stuff to do."

"What stuff?"

"Just stuff!"

"Okay. Sure. I Love you. Bye."

"Bye, Mom. I love you."

Harris put down his phone and grabbed his laptop.

A month later Harris passed a balding man carrying an ice bucket and wearing his Loneliness Conference '14 lanyard around his neck. He got the sense the man wanted to exchange pleasantries, but Harris just looked straight ahead, he needed to focus. It was an older hotel so the elevator down from the 13th floor gave Harris time to go over his first step: hit the bathroom before the earliest event, The Isolation of Modernity. He'd already gone four times that morning, but he didn't want to be the guy who has to get up and go all the time. Obviously, going to the bathroom was normal and necessary, but to do so during the first event would make him look weak. First impressions matter even at an event that according to its website was "open to all types."

On the seventh floor the elevator stopped and a woman wearing fancy looking jeans, a snug white sweater that accentuated tastefully sized breasts, and glasses that were just emo enough to be sexy, but not too emo to be intimidating or goofy, stepped inside. There were two options, well three actually. He could make pleasant, non-threatening eye contact with her in hopes that later she'd recognize him, which would make it easier to strike up a conversation. But how would he approach her? "Hello, I'm Harris and we looked at each other in the elevator earlier." The second option was to talk to her now. This was dangerous. If it went well he'd have a leg up on every other lonely dude at the conference, but the more likely outcome would be that he'd say something and she'd respond and that would be it. There was also the chance that they'd get on too well and he'd get put in The Friend Zone. Dear God that was stupid, though. Worrying about getting put in The Friend Zone during a two and a half day conference-vacation-party was borderline insane.

The last option, and the one the old Harris, the one he was changing, yesterday's Harris, would most likely do was to just pull out his phone and pretend not to look at the Glasses Girl. In the end he felt that since he'd flown all the way out to L.A. for a Loneliness Conference, there was only one choice and it was the one that involved the most sweating.

"Are you here for the conference?" he asked.

"Yep. Not a tourist."

It was off to a good start and she was looking at him.

"Yeah, me too."

Great.

"Are you with a group or are you here by yourself?" Glasses Girl asked.

Harris's "Yeah, me too" was more thought provoking than he'd realized.

"I'm just by myself. I can't imagine dragging anyone to this kind of thing. I mean, how would that conversation go?"

She laughed and introduced herself. Her name was Joyce. Traditional yet intriguing, but the name itself was immaterial. The fact that she wanted Harris to know her name was what mattered. A month of impatient waiting filled with reliving past failures and ruminations on his self-hatred and a $500 conference fee was made worthwhile by a simple introduction.

But silence filled the elevator and Joyce looked at her phone and soon they'd arrive at the lobby where all the other losers would see Joyce, his Joyce, and they wouldn't be intimidated by her glasses and they'd want to know her name and would wonder about her tastefully sized breasts just as he had. He'd made a connection with a person just like him, who also happened to be attractive, and now fate needed to meet action.

"So people come to this kind of thing in a group? That kind of defeats the purpose, though, right?" he asked.

"Not really. A lot of universities pay for trips like this. Before I left academia and went into publishing—I'm an editor for a dating advice website—I went to a few similar conferences."

"Yeah, yeah. I guess I was just –" he trailed off as the door opened.

"See you out there, Harris. I'm going to look for an old colleague, but maybe you could save me a seat."

She smiled at him as she strutted into a throng of smart jeans and plaid dress shirts. He was done. He closed the elevator door, got to the 13th floor, passed The Balding Man again, and went to find the Harris that accidentally booked a trip to an academic conference so he could kill him.

. . .

Before he knew he was a citizen of Idiotsville, USA and not just a tourist, Harris had organized his room. He'd put socks and underwear and undershirts in one drawer and some exercise clothes he'd brought for a now even more pathetic reason in another and he'd hanged some nicer clothes in the closet. His forethought and organization was his depression's coup de grace. You needed to play to win the game, but there was no point in playing a game he'd never heard of. The hotel king size bed welcomed him.

He'd been flipping between a local news station ,where they'd spent three discussing this weekend's perfect weather, and a daytime paternity test show; neither program was helping. Perfect weather was irritating because he hadn't rented a car and would have been too ashamed to go to the Hollywood Sign anyway, and paternity test shows hadn't been amusing since he was twelve, which was the last time he could take ridiculousness on TV without hating himself for watching it, or worse without seeing a bit of himself in it. Just as a well-known and ironic black and white commercial for a men's hair product began, there was a knock at the door. He got up to tell the maids they could come back later when he was out to find the nearest Arby's, but when he opened the door he saw The Balding Man, lanyard still prominent, holding two glasses of champagne in blue plastic flutes.

"Sup?" The Balding Man said.

"Can I help you?"

"Well, I just thought that since we were in the same situation that we might hang out, you know?"

"What situation is that?"

"The alone in L.A. with nothing to do situation, man. C'mon. We both got duped. Let's at least have some fun, right?" The Balding Man said as he stepped inside Harris's room.

Harris accepted the extended plastic glass of champagne without thinking, but after he took a sip he reawakened to the absurdity of the situation and wanted out as soon as possible.

"Dude, just because we're idiots doesn't mean we should celebrate," he said.

"Well, when did you find out?"

"This morning."

"Okay, that's good. Now I know what I'm working with. See I found out last night when I went down to the lobby."

"Was it obvious?"

"Yep, and I was like you. I came back to my room and just sat there for the rest of the night trying to find something to watch on TV. I ended up doing one-and-a-half regular season baseball games. That's how desperate I was. But I woke up, said 'Fuck it,' and started planning."

Harris wondered when this man would leave. When the Balding Man asked him to check out his room, he thought he could poke his head in, say it was nice to meet him, and then avoid him for the rest of the weekend.

Still punch drunk, Harris didn't have the awareness to laugh, but under normal circumstances he would have looked away or risk rudeness. There was a brand new Styrofoam cooler filled with ice, three closed and one open mid-priced champagne bottles, a twelve pack of domestic bottled beer, and a jug of orange juice. On the small table beside the television, The Balding Man had arranged some muffins, cookies, bananas and apples on paper plates. Also, there was a stack of napkins held down by the remote control. The Balding Man had rented a car and woken up early and decided to hit the grocery store and get "party supplies" in case anybody cool from the conference wanted an "escape" or if he met another person who'd been duped. Strong eye contact was made at the latter point with the addition of "It's good luck, really."

Harris still hadn't made his getaway move, or even said much at all since he'd been in The Balding Man's room. He had some time to himself while The Balding Man was in the bathroom –singing the refrain from "Hold On Loosely" by .38 Special while urinating– and realized that he was hungry and picked up a blueberry muffin. It was good. In the middle of his second bite he was hit in the back by something. He turned to see a smile and a Los Angeles Guide book on the carpet.

"Oh, I'm Jerry, by the way. You want to do this?"

...

Jerry wouldn't shut up. He began with small talk: how the best part about rental cars was the satellite radio, his surprise to learn that liquor was sold freely in California grocery stores, and the expense of the trip he took to Disney Land with his ex-wife and their two twin daughters four years ago. Traffic was stop and go and they were headed to the coast and this meant there were at least twenty-five minutes to pass before they arrived at Venice Beach.

"Yeah, and that's how I knew, man," Jerry said.

"Knew what?" Harris asked. Checking his phone's GPS every thirty seconds made focusing difficult. "I'm sorry. I didn't catch that last part."

"Oh. Okay. Well, the whole reason I came here—obviously it was an accident—was because I knew I had to do something. And do you know how I knew? Do you know how it hit me?" Jerry questioned.

Harris considered suggesting that Jerry realized the sad state of his loneliness a month ago when he was driving around Seattle with a work colleague having a one-sided conversation about how sweet it was to get satellite radio in their rented Camry.

"You know that commercial for Erziond? The erectile dysfunction medicine? The one where the dude with the deep country voice sings, 'We'll help you bond with Erziond.' Well I was walking around my apartment one night and I was just singing that to myself while I did the dishes and while I folded my laundry and all that little stuff. I was just singing 'We'll help you bond with Erziond' by myself. At first I thought it was kind of funny and then I tried to think back to when I'd last seen the advertisement, which meant that I had to remember what I'd been watching on TV and that was pretty sad in itself. In the end I couldn't recall when I'd last seen it. So that meant it was just permanently in my head. This ED commercial song. And I don't even have ED! As far as I know at least. So you see why I rushed to find something like this."

For the first time in the trip, Harris felt a genuine excuse not to respond to Jerry.

.   .   .

Mocking strangers is the easiest way for two people to connect without getting too personal, and Harris was an expert. Jerry didn't seem to realize his TV commercial talk spooked Harris, but any attempts to go deeper were blocked and attention would be directed to a Dad trying to corral his uninterested teenagers for an ocean back-dropped photo op, a super muscle-bound dude laying out unnecessarily close to the main walk way who would look up every thirty seconds to see if anyone was looking at him, or two bike cops eating ice cream. It was almost too easy.

"Okay, check out those two dudes over there," Harris said as he and Jerry walked back toward their parking lot. "Look how dressed up they are. The taller one, the one without a mustache, looks like he pressed his jeans, his plaid shirt, and tried on three different pair of glasses before he came to the beach. The beach, dude. And the other guy is just a taller version of him."

"And it's not like they're shopping at any cool stores or going to a cool bar or doing anything superficially hip.

They're just here. And they're not with girls. Or talking to them," Jerry added.

"And they won't be any time soon. They're like us, I suppose, except we didn't shame ourselves and our families by dressing up to go to the beach."

"Yeah, they're like us, but not as cool."

They spent half their almost hour and a half drive back from Venice Beach mocking Yelp reviewers and the other half having serious, reverent back and forths about the perfect restaurant for their situation. Chili's or TGI Friday's would have a soothing effect and would also be a nice F You to the conference attendees who'd have thought it "such a waste" to go to an Applebee's when there was a nice, neighborhood ethnic restaurant just down the street. That's not to say that the ethnic thing wasn't Yelped and thought over. They considered going to get real Korean BBQ in Koreatown, but after both acknowledging a more than healthy interest in getting drunk it meant the only options available to them needed to be within walking distance of their hotel. The LA Brewing Company was a few blocks away and had "decent" food options.

.   .   .

"Man, if only the people who thought of that Erziond commercial could see me now."

Jerry sighed. A sigh after a joke is a universal way to signify wanting a real conversation, and Jerry's sigh was twice as long, or one second longer, than average. That put the pressure squarely on Harris's shoulders. He could shrink, but The Loneliness Conference, the one he'd meant to attend, was really about finding one's self. Or for him: being a man. A man doesn't run away. If a longer than usual sigh means it's time for him to share, then he focuses and attempts a conversation.

When Harris began to speak, Jerry cut him off. "You know, I shouldn't have talked so much about why I'm here. It doesn't matter, really. My bad. Let's talk about something else. Hmm. Oh! Tomorrow I'm thinking we hit the Hollywood Walk of Fame and maybe the Hollywood Sign and maybe a museum if we're not too pooped. Sorry I said, 'pooped.' That's a parent word."

"It's fine, Jerry. You are a parent. And all that sounds cool, man."

.   .   .

After a discreet touch of his forehead, Harris knew the sweat was real. Hungover detective work was needed. He had slept in his clothes. He had slept in his clothes and sweated all over the bed. And when he took a quick peak above the covers and saw Jerry passed out, sitting up with a beer in his hand, he had to recognize he had slept in his clothes and sweated all over Jerry's bed.

Fishing through his pocket for his phone involved rolling over and making the bed creak, but he only found out what his hungover Sherlock routine already told him: it was a little after nine AM. Harris sneaked another look at Jerry, lanyard still present, and saw no signs of movement. He wondered which one of them passed out first. Hope desired a scenario where Jerry fell asleep and then Harris, being too drunk to walk the fifty feet to his room, deciding to curl up in the bed nearest to him. If he'd passed out first, Jerry could have watched him sleep. That wasn't possible, though. It was this: after the wings and the all beers, they came back to the hotel super drunk, drank more of Jerry's beer and champagne, watched parts of the movies running on TNT and TBS, talked, and then Jerry passed out sitting in the chair. That's how it happened. So Harris got up, avoided looking into the mirror for more than half a half a second, thought about, but didn't turn off the low volume Lynyrd Skynyrd coming from Jerry's computer speakers, and left the room.

The shower was less refreshing than he would have liked. Plus he was thirsty and at the age where anything more than four beers made his face look like he'd just come from getting his wisdom teeth removed. None of it mattered, the people at the conference weren't around and if they were, they wouldn't care about him. Right now the only important thing was free breakfast.

An empty hotel dining room with a still operational breakfast buffet is a beautiful thing. It's an unexpected, touching freedom because you deserve it though it's never expected. Overcooked eggs, underperforming biscuits, and uninspired hash browns taste fifty percent better. And the whole thing is compounded if, like Harris, just twenty minutes ago you woke up hungover in a stranger's bed, but now because you've recovered there's a renewed belief that life's sweet and anything is possible. This freedom, however, is short lived when a vaguely familiar female voice interrupts the eater mid-reflection.

Joyce sat down with her cup of coffee and smiled while Harris finished swallowing the eggs that surprisingly retained their non-mediocrity.

"So, have you recovered from your shock?" she asked accompanied with a sympathetic laugh.

Approaching Harris's predicament head on, not being too cute or coy, was the right move even if he didn't know what her angle was.

Harris told her he was recovered in full and mentioned going to Venice and the Brewery, without mentioning Jerry's name. There was some silence and he took a bite of his hash browns in an attempt to look natural, "Good hash browns." She agreed. After another brief, but indeterminate silence, Joyce asked if he'd like to go to lunch with her. Without taking even half a second to think it over, or formulate a cool sounding response, he half shouted "Yes!" The empty dining area did him no favors as his "Yes!" echoed while Joyce told him to meet her in the lobby at one pm.

Just like the too quick "Yes!" Jerry was on top of Harris before there was a moment to reflect on the Joyce situation. And the speed with which Jerry asked, "You know her?" barely allowed Harris time to recognize that Jerry was still in his clothes and still wearing the lanyard. After explaining Joyce, Jerry continued the pace and asked if he was excited about the breakfast buffet and going to check out the Hollywood Walk of Fame and John Belushi's star in a few hours. Harris, matching the pace, gave a "No." almost as quick as his "Yes!" to Joyce.

·   ·   ·

Back in the room, there was no time to consider Jerry's, "☹ LOL" text or even wonder when he and Jerry exchanged numbers, he needed to pick out an outfit. It couldn't be too formal or too casual. He needed to look cool without trying, and be clean without being too neat. It was a high wire act, equal parts exciting and terrifying. Organized clothing that once caused great self-loathing had come full circle and he could now congratulate himself on his prudence. Though the newly found self-love didn't make deciding what to wear any easier. In the end he picked nice jeans and a white polo shirt, but with sneakers for coolness.

Los Angeles' weather moved him for the first time. Perfection couldn't have been that much better. He could have been in shorts and a tee-shirt and not been too cold and he could have worn a sweater without being too hot. While thinking, almost bragging to himself, about how for the first time he didn't feel like a tourist, a voice, the feminine voice, the non-Jerry one, called out from behind him. They walked the two minutes needed to get to the Brewery in rapturous conversation about the beauty of a seventy-five degree September afternoon.

They didn't order a pitcher and Harris hadn't insisted, but rather they both ordered two different beers, which Joyce suggested would be a good idea because they could both share. Intimacy. She'd gotten up to go to the bathroom without a hint of embarrassment. More intimacy. Harris wasn't surprised when he thought about it, though. Their first interaction was on many levels uncomfortable, but he could look back on it and see that there was a genuine rapport. Combine the walk to the Brewery, the potential beer swap, her going to the bathroom, and he could see the makings of something real.

He'd gotten his second text from Jerry right as she'd sat down again. The right and the classy time to check it was when she was looking over her menu. It was similar to the first one, but longer and a bit more passive aggressive. It read, "Hoes before Bros!" Ignoring it was easy, however, because he didn't have a choice. Joyce was asking him all sorts of questions. They were the kinds of questions–deep but friendly–that no one had asked him for a long time. She wanted to know about what he was like in middle school and high school and college and what kinds of friends he had there and if he was still connected with them. She even wanted to know how often he spoke to his family members. As the conversation went longer and deeper she exposed herself, too. Her best friend in high school was named Janice and they were on the cross country team together and people called them Double J.

"Oh, I was going to ask," but she didn't finish her thought, "Check it." It was another vibration from Jerry, but this time it was a picture of Errol Flynn's star with the comment, "He supposedly had a big wang." After he checked it, he nodded at her for some unknown reason, but instead of nodding back, or continuing her question she said, "Yeah, my boyfriend's texted me a lot. I think it's because I've been traveling so much lately."

"Yeah, me too. I mean, what was your question?"

"Oh, I was wondering if it was cool if I used some of the stuff we talked about for my website. You know, the dating website? I'm going to do some pieces on loneliness and just wanted to make sure it was cool if I incorporated some of our conversation. I wouldn't use your name, obviously."

Harris said, "Yeah, that's cool," stood up, put a twenty on their table, and left The Brewery.

· · ·

As he searched for John Belushi's star, Harris realized Hollywood was gross. It didn't look cool or even seem pleasant. Squeaking breaks attacked his ears from all angles. Patches of tourists took pictures of each other with Walk of Fame stars, while avoiding the eyes of the homeless. It was all under the gaze of a billboard for a new TNT drama coming this spring called *Testimony*. This wasn't a place where dreams came to live or die, but a sweltering cocoon of unease governed by the bottom line.

The metro took twenty minutes, he'd texted Jerry "I'm coming," and there was still no response. Harris walked down Hollywood Boulevard, alternating between shamefully looking down to see what Stars were there and checking his phone, wishing to see a text from Jerry that read, "At Brad Pitt's crib. I think I clogged his toilet. Oops. Haha!"

He was halfway to an intersection and had just passed over Fran Drescher when he heard a honk that caused him to look up.

"Harris!" Jerry slowed to a stop, waving to him from his rental car. A car pulled behind him, then another, and then there was a honk and what looked like a shrug from Jerry who drove off and then pulled into a parking lot. He swung back around toward Harris who was still standing beside Fran Drescher's star.

"What star is that?" Jerry shouted from the driver seat of the rental through the rolled down passenger window.

"Fran Drescher."

"I remember liking *The Nanny* just fine."

"She was also in *This is Spinal Tap*."

"Huh. Who'd she play?"

"Oh, just this pushy record executive lady."

"Oh, right, right. Well, it sounds like she's got more range than most people would realize."

Harris couldn't take any more shouting, especially shouting about an old sit com star's range as an actress, so he opened the passenger door and stepped inside.

"How was lunch with that lady? Joyce, right?" Jerry asked before Harris could contemplate explaining, or just suggesting they go do something fun where the lunch wouldn't have to be mentioned.

"It was just okay," Harris responded.

"I understand. Well, you know I was thinking about heading to the Hollywood sign. You can park and then walk up behind it. What do you think?"

"Let's do it. Let's go."

SAND CASTLES
JIM DOERING

It is her warm dimpled smile I crave, and it lights up everyone around her. She chases me across the beach, I shriek and scamper away, but she is too quick and catches me. She wraps her arms around me and covers me like a blanket before we both fall to the sand, laughing. When we sit up, she hugs me close, my face buried in the softness of her breasts, and she holds me, my tiny arms encircling her waist. Later, we sit together while she reads, and we talk of small things while sandpipers forage in the sand in front of us. When I look into her eyes she smiles again, and it is almost enough to hide the sadness that seeps out in tiny increments when she thinks nobody is watching.

Near us, an old man in a floppy hat sits on a canvas-and-wood chair painting a picture comprised mostly of yellows and shades of blue, my favorite color. He holds a coffee can full of dirty water clenched tightly between his legs, and he dips his brush-tip into it before he switches colors. He watches as my mother and I lay together on our towels, basking in the sun, the gentle ocean breeze in our faces. Once in awhile I lift my head and glance over to see if he is still looking. Later I run over to see his creation. He has painted the beach, and in the center are mother and son, walking together and holding hands. He turns to me, smiles, and goes back to working his brush across the large canvas.

I return to my mother and dig, using a bucket and shovel made out of metal. I dump buckets of moist sand in a circle around me. They become the bricks and mortar of my castle. I dig out the area inside to make the walls seem higher. Prickly points of sand cling to my legs from sweat on the hot Long Island summer day. I ask my mother to come inside so I can protect us both from harm, but she only smiles briefly and goes back to her book, and her smile fades.

She soon announces it is time to go, picks up our things and we walk side-by-side to our car just on the other side of the dune. She speaks to me of things I do not completely understand. When we pull away, I watch the ocean tide gently lapping at the shore from the rear window of the car, and I wonder if I have built my fortress safely back far enough on the beach, where the water will not nibble away and steal it, bit by bit.

At home she makes tea and says her father is coming to see us. When he arrives I notice a packed suitcase sitting by the front door. Stacked on top is my sleep-time companion, Fido, a tan and brown stuffed dog. She says goodbye to me, holding me an extra-long time that for some reason makes me uncomfortable, and when I leave with her father, riding in the back seat of his car, I hold on to Fido tightly as she waves from the porch, her smile absent. By the time we arrive at his home, somehow her father has become my father, his family is now mine, and my mother has lost hers.

. . .

My older sister is screaming. I have just come into the house, home from kindergarten, pretending to have driven home from work in a blue pedal car on the backyard sidewalk that looks just like Dad's Chevy Bel Air. My sister is almost hysterical and yells something about someone trying to break into our house and that she needs to call the police. She picks up the phone which sits on a small wooden table at the entry to our house at the bottom of the stairs and yells at the lady on the party-line to hang up because this is an emergency. From behind her I see a face peeking in the living room window. The man's eyes dart around looking inside the house, and then the face disappears. A man in an untucked white shirt flashes across our lawn. After she hangs up, my sister turns to me and says, "Your father was here to kidnap you. Don't worry, the police will catch him." I am confused because my father is at work, just like always, and there is no reason the police should be after him. I never see the white-shirted man again.

. . .

My dad likes to make things out of wood, and he is teaching me how. One Christmas I receive a set of tools inside a small, metal toolbox. They are miniature versions of his. He takes me down into the basement where he keeps his meticulously organized workbench and shows me how to use my new tools. We spend hours together bending and shaping wood to our respective wills. He glances periodically at me as I work at a small table he built for me to use near his workbench. I am trying to hammer a nail straight into a piece of scrap wood while he carefully sands the arms of a chair. A cigarette hangs from the side of his mouth, and smoke rises from the lit end, curling its way up to his right eye, which makes it partially close. When I finally get the nail all the way down into the wood, I hold it up to show him, and he smiles back, showing his approval. The smoke in his eye makes it look like he is winking at me.

. . .

It is a bright and sunny Saturday morning. I set up plastic army men on the concrete floor near my dad's workbench. I have just completed the fortifications that protect the Americans from the Germans when I hear rapidly moving footsteps on the hardwood floor above me. My sister comes down the stairs and tells me my father has been taken away in an ambulance. He has died from the cancer ravaging his body. I stare at her, unblinking. I want to cry, but for some reason I cannot. After the funeral my adopted mother tells me I am now the man of the family and that I was a good boy because I did not cry in front of anyone. She tells me that men do not cry because they are strong. Three weeks before I had celebrated my tenth birthday in a hospital waiting room opening a present from my father, a new pair of skates, while he lay unconscious in a nearby room. I was told he was too sick for me to thank him for his perfect gift.

. . .

I sit in a front-row desk in my eighth grade math class. I do not like my teacher, who is mean, but I love math, and I am also looking forward to my next class period, a film club elective. A strange old woman is visiting our class and embarrassingly singles me out. The rest of the class sitting behind me enjoys my humiliation as the stranger touches my hair before walking to the door to leave. My teacher tells me the old woman needs to speak to me in the hallway. When the door closes behind us I am expecting an apology, but instead the woman says she is my grandmother and that her son, my real father, has been murdered. I tell her she is crazy, because my father died three years before from cancer, but somewhere inside me a door has been unlocked, and I remember my mother's smile and the strange man with the untucked white shirt tangled with other memories long forgotten. She tries to convince me to leave school with her in that moment and go with her to another city, but I tell her no, I have school, and I go back into math class. Later, she walks up and down the aisles of the darkened auditorium during my film class while a black-and-white movie plays. She searches for me in the flickering silver light.

. · ·

I am told we have a visitor. I call in sick to my job at the restaurant and tell my friends I will miss my team's roller hockey league game. Riding in the car, I listen as my mother tells the dimpled woman with the sad eyes how wonderful my life is, the wonderful gifts I received for my sixteenth birthday, my good grades, how happy I am, how much better a mother she has been than her daughter who is my birth-mother, and how she will soon send me off to college to become someone great. Almost none of the things she says are true, except for my grades. I sit in the back hoping these things will come to pass, but knowing in my heart they will not.

I am not allowed to call my birth mother, *Mom*. It was explained to me that if I do it would hurt my adopted mother's feelings, so I don't use any name for either of them. At our house I sit in the kitchen as my birth-mother talks on the telephone. I watch as she nods her head in answer to a question on the other end of the line while sitting in a vinyl chair next to the Formica table in our kitchen. I have not seen her in thirteen years, and I watch her doodling on a blank pad of paper while she talks. A cigarette hangs from the side of her mouth, and the smoke curls up into her eyes, causing it to close. I walk over to see what she is drawing. It is a three-mast sailing ship. I haven't let anyone ever see my drawings, including the one I drew six months earlier of an almost identical three-mast ship.

It is soon time for her to leave. I hug her and say goodbye at the airport gate, and for a moment I see the eyes that I remember have grown sadder. As she walks down the hallway, I remember I forgot to ask her why she has dimples and I do not.

.   .   .

In college I fall quickly in love with an artist. She is talented, passionate and emotional, all things I think I am not. We spend hours telling each other everything about ourselves, and we hold each other tightly in her dorm room bed to insulate ourselves from the world. I tell her about my father and our making things out of wood together and am surprised when I am overcome with grief that seems to be never-ending. It occurs to me I have not wept over anything since his death. My girlfriend pulls me close, cries along with me and pledges to love me forever.

She gives me paintings and drawings as gifts for Christmases, birthdays and anniversaries. After a fight between us two years later, I come home to an empty house. She is gone and has taken all my paintings and drawings with her. Shortly after, I receive a call from my mother telling me my birth-mother died from chronic lung disease six months earlier. There was no funeral.

·   ·   ·

Many years have passed since, and I find myself reflecting back when I cannot get to sleep. It feels sometimes like someone else has lived the life I remember, and I have simply been a spectator. As the years have floated by, I have the palpable sense that the light of these memories is fading, like a star in the night sky which burns brightly and gradually twinkles out.

Sometimes I dream I am back on the beach making sand castles, and the tide is washing closer. As the sun slowly sets beyond the horizon and the day comes to an end, I am back on that sunny beach, standing alone.

From time to time I think back on the picture painted by the old man at the beach on that beautiful, long-ago summer day. I wonder if the two figures walking together in the painting are still there or have instead faded from view, leaving nothing but the beach and a long-abandoned sand castle, built to keep the two of them safe from all the evil in the world.

MIRIAM'S SONG
LARRY LEFKOWITZ

Until our tenth birthday, my sister and I were one person. Fraternal twins, our closeness was not hindered, but enhanced, by our difference in gender. Our thoughts were as one thought. Since we could feel what the other was thinking, we had no need to speak. It was not until our third birthday that we spoke our first words, and then at the same time according to our mother, "Only because you had to communicate with the outside world," by which she meant the rest of the family. When reminded by the shtetl women about our slowness in speaking—for signs of intelligence were eagerly sought in shtetl children and speaking early was one of them—she would reply, "Why should they speak? They speak to each other without speech. Even after they learned to speak, they talked with their father and me less than other children talk with their parents." It was clear that she felt apart, especially from her daughter whom it was her duty to train in the ways of the home. As for me, Miriam, my sister, my twin, was more a mother to me.

We preferred our own company to that of other children. On the infrequent occasions when we joined their games, we had their advantage. In hide-and-seek we knew where the other was hiding and would mentally warn of whoever was "it". And when one of us was "it", we never "found" the other person—that was an unspoken rule, like all our rules. The game, like everything we did, was our conspiracy against the rest of the world, against our parents, against everything that was not us.

We were the darlings and the mystery of the shtetl. Adam and Eve we were called, since we seemed each a part of the other.

While I learned Torah, Miriam, as a girl groomed for the home was taught only a few prayers, yet she knew as much as I did, to the astonishment of everyone but us. Whatever I learned was absorbed by her simultaneously. When I was honored with a ceremony on completion of my studies, I felt that she felt she had earned it, too. The residents of the shtetl began to call us "Double Ayin" for the Hebrew verbs where the two same letters coming together are written as one letter. "Hello, Double Ayin," they would say, whether addressing me, or Miriam, or us together.

In the eyes of the shtetl, our most amazing feat was our ability to suddenly start singing the same song at the same time without previous signal, even if we started in the middle instead of at the beginning, as we sometimes did. In this we were like the shofars of Reb Zalman and Reb Elya: if one was blown , the other would reverberate.

Our closeness continued, two magnets in each other's pull, until our tenth birthday. On this birthday, as on every one that had gone before, we received gifts we considered ours rather than mine, but then, at 10 o'clock in the morning—so vividly is it fixed in my memory—it happened. We were sitting in the kitchen, nibbling on the after breakfast snacks left by mother to tide us over from breakfast to lunch, when my twin began singing a song I had never heard, a song without words. Although I had never heard the melody before, it was not the melody that turned my blood to ice. She was singing *alone*, and not because I chose not to join in: *I hadn't felt the song*. I could only stare at her, numbed into a speechlessness that was the first borne of our failure to communicate, and if she was aware of my surprise (as I have no doubt that she was), she showed no sign, refusing even to send me an explanation. From that moment, we were two people instead of one.

Each day our separation increased, gradual though it was. It did not involve hostility on the part of my sister, it was simply her refusal to share—an absence, rather than a conflict—a withholding of herself that grew. In the beginning, I implored her with my thoughts, "What has happened? Why?" but she closed off her mind to me. It was as if she had died, and yet she had not died, or rather, her soul had died and her body had lived. "What happened to the Double Ayin?" people asked. "They are growing up," mother answered. "One's a boy and the other's a girl, they have different interests." She believed this explanation, and so did everyone else. People began to call us by our separate names.

Miriam would sing none of the old songs, only that wordless song which was the first she refused to share, walking to it in the slow steps of a pavan; and if I was present, to her it was as if I was not there.

Except for the song, she became silent—not only to me, which had always been so, we never needed words—but to others. Her behavior was so noticeably different that the shtetl began to contrast her conduct to mine, treating us as different instead of the same — to the praise of me and the criticism of her. But I felt no glow in their praise ... I had now become one of them, and Miriam was alone. What made me despair was her refusal to be aware of my solitude: for her to have known how I felt and yet refuse reconciliation would have been painful, but that she refused to *know* how I felt left me struggling to hold on to my sanity.

In addition to her silence, Miriam began to sleep during the day, to the distraction of a mother whose imploring concerns were met with a silence on the part of her daughter, as if she had not heard her questions. At night, Miriam would walk through the house, sometimes silent, sometimes singing the song, which by now was called "Miriam's song."

I would watch her in her sleep-like walk, as devoted to her as she was oblivious to my presence. When I placed myself in her path, she walked around me in her slow, dignified pavan, as if I were a chair which had been moved from its accustomed place. There came upon me the temptation to grab her, to stop her, to clamp my hand over her mouth to end the song—futile as this would have been since it seemed to emanate from her even when she was silent, as though the song had replaced that part of her that once was me. But I never did. Something restrained me, perhaps the fear of losing her for good, or of her turning on me physically—something she had never done—and which I could not live with.

If Miriam was not already the object of whispers in the shtetl, her conduct of which I am now to speak, made her so. She would leave the house at night to walk within the shtetl singing her song as she used to walk within the house, as though she refused any longer to be confined by its walls. My mother was fearful when she learned of this: What would the shtetl think? And in truth the shtetl women began to murmur "Lilith" when they saw her.

Unable to sleep, I worried. Miriam's song would enter my mind at night, when she was singing it and when she wasn't—the song seemed as much a part of me as of her, the only part of her that still was, but in an unwanted way, for I never felt myself singing it with her; she alone sang it in my mind, a song that divided us, that kept her separate from me.

In the family's desperation, the decision was made to consult the Tsaddik. When he sent for her, Miriam did not resist, walking to his residence beside me as unaware of my presence as when she walked at night, her shadow more real than the figure at my side. And it was precisely this conduct which was so remarkable and so frightening: Miriam did not resist our efforts to "cure" her (this was the word my mother used) but neither did she respond to them. Like wheat brushed with a stick, she yielded without yielding, remaining unchanged.

She did not resist when the Tsaddik led her into his study like a submissive bride. It was forbidden to listen through the door, yet I could not refrain from doing so, a former part of me—a part I despaired of regaining—was inside. Behind the closed door, silence prevailed for the half hour that passed before I heard the Tsaddik's footsteps. I hurriedly retreated from the door, though it was not necessary; "Silence cannot be heard through a door," the Tsaddik said to me without anger, and in the same tone, "I can do nothing; she is beyond our help, for there is something that cannot be found in any place, not even with the Tsadik, yet there is a place that you will find it." The Tsaddik's face was perplexed; Miriam's bore the same distant look as when she had entered.

Mother wept openly for twenty-four hours when I told her the words of the Tsaddik, as I wept inwardly for so much longer.

It was my uncle who suggested it. Not from a willingness to help her so much as an attempt to get rid of her since, as one of the leaders of the community, he suffered from the shtetl's incessant talk of Miriam's "condition"—and implicitly, the lack of anyone's doing anything about it—more than the rest of the family. "Surely the place hinted at by the Tsadik is the Land of Israel. Perhaps the climate there will aid her," he said, as if she suffered from tuberculosis. Even I chose to think of Miriam's condition as an illness: it removed the volition from her separation from me. The Land of Israel was espoused by the Lovers of Zion, and though my uncle did not hide his disapproval of the youth going there, in my sister's case—for reasons of health—he was willing to make an exception.

My mother reluctantly agreed, at panic's end about her daughter. I, too, was willing to seize at any hope, any chance, to reunite my sister to me. I was given the task of taking Miriam to the Land of Israel, to one of the settlements in the Galilee where sun and work would be allowed to heal.

The settlement caused a slight improvement in Miriam, if an improvement in body, not mind. She became physically healthier—so that she worked during the day rather than slept and continued her night walks, now with the strength to do both. I, too, had benefited from coming to the Land of Israel. The pain of estrangement from my sister was not lessened, yet I was no longer kept awake by her song. I was dimly aware of it, but it remained below the surface, only occasionally troubling me with its seductive melody.

Otherwise there was no change: Miriam remained apart from me, and from the settlers, an isolation which they accepted; they were tolerant of an individual's habits so long as he or she was a good worker. If they wondered about her night wanderings and singing, they said nothing, for this was a peaceful time and there was then no hostility with the Arabs in neighboring villages to render her excursions dangerous.

It was to one of these villages to which she would walk, singing her song, as I learned from following her. Not an Arab village, but a village of Yemenite Jews near the Sea of Galilee. In the village, she would stop before a certain house, no different from the houses surrounding it. She would stand gazing at it for long periods as if waiting for someone to emerge from it, but no one emerged, nor did she enter. The inhabitants sleeping inside seemed unaware of her presence, all the more so the other villagers. If they saw her on the occasions when I did not follow her—unlike my sister, I had not the strength both to work and wander—I had no knowledge. Perhaps, like the inhabitants of the shtetl, they thought her an evil spirit and remained behind locked doors when she approached. When I did not follow her, I knew it was to this same house that she went. I envied the house for the attention of Miriam that had once been mine.

For I was no closer to her without whom I only half existed. My despair increased as the possibility of being reunited to her seemed ever more remote, since she continued to treat me with the same indifference she showed to other members of the settlement. Suicidal thoughts tormented me. If I could have been sure that my death would have caused her to shed even one tear—I would have taken my life. Doubting, I did not act.

During the second year that we dwelled in the Land of Israel, at the fall season of harvesting the apple crop, there occurred a slight change in Miriam. She became less remote from everyone in the settlement, except that her remoteness from me persisted. She spoke a bit more, and her secret—for the settlers suspected that she kept some secret, and I, myself, had come to wonder if indeed she did not—seemed less burdensome. There was now an expectancy about her, and a tension as if caused by her straining toward it, the effort of which pulled her partially free of her somnolence.

One night after dinner, as I lay back watching the stars, thinking, as I thought each time I looked at them, how different they were from the stars above the shtetl—the ones my sister and I used to follow, tracing the constellations with our eyes and thought and laughing our conspiratorial laugh whenever we came to the Twins—my sister approached me in her silent way. Concentrating as I was that moment on tracing the Water Carrier, I was not immediately aware of her presence. When I sensed her standing there, I jumped up, amazed at this first sign of recognition after so long a time, my heart beating so strongly I felt like a lover who first sees his beloved after an intolerable absence. I was about to reach out to her, to gather her to me, when her hand on my shoulder stopped me, so gentle her touch that I was grateful for it alone even in my sorrow at her not allowing me more. But it was her expression, the same a fawn has when it is listening for something, that prevented me from attempting to bridge a gap greater than separated me from the stars. And then I, too, heard the song. It did not come from Miriam, but from a flute somewhere out in the darkness, distant, the sound growing louder as its source approached.

Miriam turned to face it as if expecting it, looked back at me for an instant—the fawn changed to Lot's wife caught in the moment of her forbidden look back at Sodom—then her face became submissive again and she moved in her silent pavan toward the sound. The figure playing it appeared, his face dark, his features not recognizable in the moonless night. He stopped as she approached him, turned, still playing, the two shadows merging into one glided down the path toward the village. I took a step toward them, toward my twin who was not my twin, but a slight movement of her finger, discernable from his only by its slimness I knew better than my own finger, made without her turning her head or even slowing her step, stopped me. I knew she would not hesitate this time outside the house in the village. I knew, too, as I felt the song being pulled out of me forever, that in fusing her soul with another's, she had freed my own.

WATCHING THE HOMELESS
ALAN WRIGHT

We lived in a little town underneath the redwoods in northern California. We'd been married a couple of years and had moved around before settling into a fairly easy way of living. Like a lot of northern CA, it is both idyllic and psychotic, the inhabitants are beautiful and haggard, the sun shines in between bouts of fog, and the forests give shelter to the many transients and homeless people who find their way beneath the canopy and never leave.

The open field behind our apartment was where they settled and played during the day. It was close to town and the grocery store. They'd come back with 40s of Cobra, never enough for a full day, just a couple at a time, pacing themselves. They'd drink liquor as the sun receded behind the clouds. Those with children would head off to the one shelter in town; the others would slip off into the woods for a night of drinking and fighting, eventually crawling into the bushes and their makeshift shelters.

I played guitar in the back bedroom, looking out the window, watching the daytime drama unfold and play out in front of me. I was in between jobs and feeling bad my wife was doing all the work while I stayed home and cleaned, drank and played guitar. I did whatever I could to avoid the writing I told myself I was going to do, that I told myself I couldn't do while holding down a job. Watching them made me feel better about myself.

Living right beside a huge stand of redwoods, we often went for walks. One day we discovered an outdoor church. Right there in a clearing. Pews cut from thick redwood, enough for a good sized parish, a stage and alter carved from stone and trees. The earth hard and clear of leaves, needles and the detritus of a shedding forest. It was bare and humble, sacred in its austerity. We wandered aimlessly, touching everything as we passed. We walked the aisles in separate directions, occasionally passing and touching hands, smiling.

We met again by the altar, facing each other and stopped. We looked into each other's eyes and then up towards the sky. It had taken on an afternoon grey and as I looked up through the clearing, it looked as if the trees brushed right up against it. I kept staring, holding her hands and feeling her heart beat. The difference between the clouds above me and the dirt I was standing on, started to lose its footing. I let it slide as I closed my eyes and felt it hum. So much bigger than anything I could imagine. We were so much bigger than anything I could imagine.

I felt myself starting to tilt over backwards, and from the pulling on my hands I could tell she was, too. I opened my eyes to see her laughing as she started to pull us into a spin, I pulled her to me and wrapped her in my arms, never breaking eye contact, at least not until we started to kiss. But that was only for a minute, and then we were laughing and running into the woods, chasing each other down the root broken trail, jumping over rocks and hiding behind trees. We stumbled through a soft patch of dirt and tumbled over each other into some hollowed out low lying brush.

We sat, panting and giggling, while I pulled out the joint I had rolled before the walk. She leaned over and kissed my neck before resting her head on my shoulder as I lit and inhaled, breathing in deep before holding it to her lips and letting her do the same. We did that for a while, letting our heartbeats settle and our breathing slow. I laid my head on hers and closed my eyes, enjoying the quiet moment.

When I opened my eyes, I was looking into the entrance of a larger deeper hollowed out area. I could see what looked like fabric and crumpled bits of paper and plastic bags. I slid around her with a "hey baby, look over here" and crawled through the opening. Inside was a typical makeshift shelter. It wouldn't stop a hard rain, but it kept most prying eyes out at night. There was the usual trash and cast offs: blankets, toilet paper, old beer cans, some clothing and other various remnants of a life in constant transition.

I first remember my grandfather when I was 7 years old. My dad had died and we were spending a lot of time with my mother's parents. They lived at the beach, in the woods. My grandfather spent most of the day in his easy chair watching the 4 channels they got, while my grandmother chain smoked and listened to the radio. My skin crawled, sitting on the two steps leading down from their kitchen to the living room while golf blared through the static UHF, fighting the classical music emanating from the little speakers and haze of parliaments. I started sneezing shortly after our arrival. My mom lamented the dampness of the trees. The walls and curtains bled brown from cigarette smoke, but we were worried about the trees.

Retired, my grandfather worried about growing sedentary. He went for long walks, and I followed, begging him to tell his impossible stories about Indians and settlers and soldiers and the like, fantasies that extended past the usual TV drama I had grown to believe was real. He filled the regular world with mystery and danger. Every step we took potentially revealed a civil or revolutionary war relic, the Indians and cowboys were everywhere.

Sitting in this hovel, I realized I had come upon many a homeless hovel during my travels with my grandfather. He pointed them out as teepees, or the burned out shelters of soldiers, sometimes they were just adventurers living off the land. They certainly weren't modern casualties, trying to find shelter from the storm.

I unfurled one of the balled up pieces of paper, smoothing it out against my knee so I could decipher the scrawling. "Im so sorry baby I know I shouldnt of left you. I know its my falt I'm sittin here in lok up, but you gota no I love you. You wait for me I'll be there and we'll finily be together agin. Ill stay clean and you wont have to worry about what Im gonna do. You can forgive me. That will never happen agin. I'm sorry. I promise. I'm sorry." It kept going, more sadness and mayhem.

She crawled in next to me and read it, too. I tried to pull it away from her, but she grabbed my hand and read it anyway.

She looked up at me, "Why are you reading this?'

Because it makes me feel better.

"I don't know, I'm just curious, you know? Look at this, I mean, what drives you to be this way and end up here."

"I don't know, but it feels private, I wouldn't want anyone reading anything like this that I wrote. Just put it down, and let's leave."

I tossed it back in the corner and we crawled out of the bush in silence.

It was the kind of silence that makes me uncomfortable. Most silence does, but this was particular. We walked anyway, next to each other, close but not hand in hand. The glow, the vibrancy, the life that seemed imbued in everything was replaced with grey melancholy. I knew I needed to say something, but just as strongly I knew whatever I would say would be wrong, so I walked instead.

That's me, the strong silent type.

"You ok?"

I looked at her from the side of my face, hoping she would just say yes and I could relax. She didn't answer, but she reached out and grabbed my hand, her eyes still fixed on the path in front of us. We walked like that for a while, covering the ground, putting distance between us and it.

"Why did you have to read that?"

"What do you mean? I didn't have to, it was just there; it was interesting. You know? Like being an archeologist."

"But it's not like that. We weren't uncovering some sacred past, it was the sad history of someone living right now. I wish I'd never seen it. I wish you would have just left it alone."

I was a blank slate. I knew I should feel bad, but I didn't, so I wasn't sure how to respond in a way that would make her feel ok, so I didn't say anything. I just kept walking.

"Didn't it make you feel uncomfortable? Reading their private life?"

It made me feel so much better than I did before I read it, even better than when we kissed. "I don't know. I didn't really think about it that way, I mean I guess I did. I felt sad for them, you know? I felt so lucky, too. So lucky it was them, and not me."

She took her hand from mine.

"Of course it isn't you."

"Well of course it isn't me, I'm standing right here, but I mean, what if it was? It just as well could be, as much as it could be anyone else."

"No it couldn't. That's fucking ridiculous. Of course you're not going to be homeless and living in the woods. What kind of crazy shit would have to happen for you to end up there? That's not even the point; the point is what are you going to do about it? Can you really just pretend like it's not happening after reading that letter?"

That was when my head started to pound. Fuck. All I wanted was some fun in the woods, get a little high, maybe get laid, move on to the next thing. Instead I'm supposed to be figuring out my philanthropic contribution to the world. God dammit. I can't think about contributing anything. I love her for her incredulity at the notion, such faith. She says it like she knows me on a level I don't, and it's that knowledge, her knowledge, that makes me think maybe it's true, and maybe it's utterly stupid to think someone like me could end up like someone like them.

We kept walking and I slipped my hand in hers. She took it gently, with a familiarity that warmed my heart in a way nothing else could. I knew right then and there that all those little demons boiling up inside of me had no place to go. Her hand in mine was all it took to hold them back and break their spell. I knew, as I walked out into the clearing, nothing could do me any harm.

I continued to hold her hand as we walked back to our apartment; I knew I'd never consider living in a fucking bush. I knew I was responsible and ambitious, I knew I was driven. Hell, most of the problems we'd had were because I worked too much, there was no way in hell I'd ever live in a bush.

We walked on up the flight of steps and into our place; we made a simple dinner, eating it with a bottle of wine before making it to bed. She slept her quiet little sleep, her head on my shoulder as I lay there, reciting part of the letter like counting sheep.

"I'm sorry, I'm sorry" over and over again.

UGLY AS SIN
JEFFREY SYKES

Derrick was outside because he wanted a cigarette, some fresh air and to walk off the third erection Mary's bare thighs had given him during the Christmas cantata's first act.

He slipped from his chair at the end of the balcony's third row and was around the exit and to the steps before Todd, his best friend who'd dated Mary for two months now, looked up from where his fingers rested entwined with Mary's, his wrist brushing against the charms dangling from her tennis bracelet.

There were a few older couples moving through the vast concrete lobby at Reynolds Auditorium, but no adults from the church leadership or those involved with the youth group. So Derrick passed through the double doors and into the freedom of a December night.

He followed the walkway around the side of the auditorium to avoid being detected once he lit the filtered Camel, enjoying the pungent aroma as the smoke hit his nostrils for the first time. He'd just flicked the match onto the erect winter grass, frozen in place by one of those sudden cold snaps that visits central North Carolina before the mild winters set in, when he saw two people coming down the side walkway.

He turned back toward the front of the auditorium and caught sight of a crescent moon just below Orion's sword held in the distance.

"Derrick! What's going on?"

It was Jeff Pyrtle, another youth group member. Beside him Kevin Ballance, the pastor's eldest son. "Still smoking those things?" Jeff said. "I thought you'd made a prayer request last month for help to stop?"

Derrick pulled on the filter and deeply inhaled the smoke before blowing it high into the vacant night.

"Kind of tough," he said. "What are you dudes doing out here?"

"We're heading back to the church," Kevin said. "Trey wants us to get the PA working in the gym so it will be ready for tomorrow."

The youth group had grown very large. Much larger than when Derrick first started years earlier while still in fifth grade. His middle school group had maybe twenty kids, but once he hit high school the youth group exploded as the church grew weekly until it became the largest, most visible church in town. Its prominent position at a major intersection across from Wake Forest University didn't hinder the progress.

The youth group had outgrown the classrooms, even the new areas of the church that spread out from the original building on both sides like angel wings.

Jeff turned to walk, and Derrick followed him down the long sidewalk leading to the parking lot. He would walk to the end and finish his cigarette, and then turn back to look for Todd and Mary to see if they wanted to bail.

"Who's the new girl Todd's with?" Kevin asked him.

"Man is she ugly," Jeff said.

"Ugly as sin," Kevin replied.

Derrick was stunned as he pulled the Camel from his lips. But he was in no mood to argue and so he replied in a flat tone that masked his shock and anger.

"Her name's Mary. She lives in Buena Vista. I guess they met in class or something."

Derrick stopped walking. "I like her a lot. She's a nice person."

He turned without speaking and walked back toward the steps leading to the concert hall's entrance. Pausing at the base of the steps, he looked back to Orion. Dots of light forming a pattern interpreted ages before. He liked to look at the stars and try and find his own patterns, but none ever came. So he contented himself with the structure of the heavens.

He'd long ago grown tired of Christians. Their patterns bored him. But he liked the shape of any number of the girls he'd grown up with in the church. Girls now turning to women all around him. Todd could have his pick of the bunch. It'd been that way since they first became friends six years earlier, meeting on a ball field, talking about sports during Sunday school, growing closer on sleepovers or day trips with their families.

Todd was his best friend. They'd been inseparable for years, even now that they each had their own car, their own job and their own pocket money. Todd even had an attractive girlfriend, their pair merely became three of a kind. Everyone knew they were like brothers, especially the pastor's son Kevin. He was a year younger, but he'd played countless hours of basketball with them and an equal amount in church pews, or classrooms, talking game or girls. He knew what he was doing calling Mary ugly in front of Derrick. Todd would hit the roof.

.   .   .

Derrick had seen Mary around the high school halls before she began dating his best friend. She was a pretty girl with a sweet mouth, pursed lips like a ripe plum. She was small and thin and oh so feminine. Her dresses and dangling bracelets helped her cut a swath of womanhood among the girls at school still wearing jeans and tennis shoes.

She lived in one of those neighborhoods full of large homes near the university, while Todd lived in a small apartment complex next to a public housing project. Derrick's parents were divorced now and he lived with his mom in a small ranch just outside the city limits.

Derrick was surprised at the suddenness of Todd's fall for Mary. Overnight they'd gone from spending their afternoons finding a basketball game or getting a burger and fries, to timing their freedom to Mary's whims.

But they'd not cast him off. Quite the opposite. Mary was engaging, and Derrick enjoyed their conversations about music and friends, or where they might go to school in less than two years. Todd's parents were very strict with his comings and goings. His dad was a deacon at the church and prone to making the loudest amen shouts at least once a Sunday.

Derrick didn't realize at first that he was Todd's cover story. But as the fall progressed, and the routines became established, he adjusted and played his role as protector of his friend's private time like a champ.

At first it amounted to little more than keeping up appearances, showing up to take Todd to the rec center to play basketball, chatting with Todd's mom about school and grades and the looming SATs, and then taking Todd to Mary's. He'd always try to leave, to give them space to be alone, but it was Mary who would beg him to stay.

Over the course of several weeks, they had all grown very close. Mary only recently began to come to church with Todd, where he was even more popular than at school, and she'd caused quite the stir among the gossip chain. Derrick was the one left to field many questions about her, mostly from girls who attended other high schools across the city. Most were harmless questions about her name, where she lived, what she was like.

Kevin and Jeff were fully aware of this.

. . .

Back in the auditorium's lobby, he looked for Todd and Mary and saw them coming from the balcony steps. Mary spotted him, waved her hand and smiled. She was far from ugly. Her dirty blond hair hugged her oval face and bounced with her stride. Her light pink makeup like pastel on the canvass of her rich brown skin.

She had a toothy grin, perhaps the one flaw he could account for, but the sparkle in her hazel eyes attracted his attention. Her pouty mouth was to die for. "How can anybody think she's ugly?" he thought. "What's ugly is all these fake people pretending to be holy, hiding their fears and hates behind a lie."

He must have looked disturbed as Todd and Mary approached.

"What's the matter babe?" she asked.

"Nothing, just bored."

"You look ready to fight somebody man," Todd said. "Cheer up dude, it's Christmas."

"Yeah, you're right. It's just–I get bored with this scene lately. With this repetition."

"I know what you need," Mary said. "A girlfriend. Who do we know Todd?"

"Now, now, hold up," Derrick said. "I'm content enjoying your happiness for the moment."

"Just don't get too attached," Todd said.

"Now you two don't fight," Mary said. "We can just be happy together. Are you guys about ready to go back to my parent's house? Mom picked up a couple of movies for us at Blockbuster today."

Todd and Mary walked along in front of him on the way to the car. They had all come in Derrick's Oldsmobile, he thought about saying something about the insult as he reached to unlock the passenger door and let them into the spacious back seat. But he didn't want to spoil Mary's night, or cause trouble for his friend. He knew well that Todd would get angry if told what Jeff and Kevin had said.

He was silent on the short drive back to Mary's home, where they often passed an evening in the basement watching movies. Derrick had been able to buy a six pack of beer at the Shell station near the university. He easily passed for a college student because he was well over six feet tall. He'd bought beer there several times despite being just a few months passed his sixteenth birthday.

It was cold in the basement and Mary had asked Derrick to come sit on the couch with her and Todd. "You've got to keep this side warm," she said while lifting the edge of the quilt as he slid underneath.

Just as he got settled she asked him to hand her the beer can on the table in front of them. He leaned forward and took the can and handed it to her, their fingers touched for a moment and she glanced at him with those large hazel eyes before leaning back into Todd.

"Okay, babe, start it again," she said.

The movie was a teen romance about a poor girl and a rich guy and her poor friend who gets his feelings hurt when she no longer wants to pal around with him after school, opting instead for the rich guy's car and house parties. She ended up feeling slighted in her new scene and pouted in isolation from both suitors, until she forgives the rich guy, the poor friend absolves her and she disappears into a Hollywood ending with her Romeo. In a brief denouement, the poor friend is seen catching the eye of a cute blonde attracted to his sartorial panache.

Todd excused himself as the credits rolled to pass what remained of his two beers. As he rounded the corner, Mary leaned across Derrick to put her beer can on the end table. She lingered, with her erect nipple pressed into his forearm, before she withdrew. He shifted in discomfort as Mary adjusted the quilt, moving her hands below the downy thickness.

But she didn't stay still. She moved her hand across Derrick's leg until her fingers wrapped around his penis.

"What are you doing?" he gasped.

"Shh, babe. Be still. I just had to know if I was right. I see the way you look at me," she whispered. "You're a sweet boy, Derrick. Don't play seconds to anyone."

She kissed his cheek and pulled her hand away, straightening the quilt nice and flat this time. Todd came back in a moment and said he needed to get home.

"I'll wait outside," Derrick said. He shifted clumsily to hide the lingering excitement, covering it with his wadded jacket as he moved for the basement door.

"Bye, babe. See ya tomorrow maybe?"

"Yeah, have a good night. Thanks for the movie and stuff."

Outside he waited before starting the car, hoping the winter air would cool him off.

It did not.

SEXTING IS SUCH A BAD HABIT
NIKITA HERNANDEZ

My phone vibrated in my pocket for the eighteenth time that Friday night. Emerson's name flashed across the screen. He was really intent on trying to hook up with me. He had been since the end of English Comp I last fall, after we both admitted a mutual interest in each other. I flicked my phone open and read the text message.

Hey you, it read. He never used my name. Not once had he ever said my name. It was only two syllables, *Leah*. Not a mouthful like Katarzyna or Sigourney. Emerson only texted me when he wanted to get off, so I knew this would be no friendly catch-up conversation. I pretended to be friendly and asked what was up. He quickly texted back.

Nothing really, I'd expected you to text me sometime, just haven't heard from you, kind of worried.

I last texted him earlier in the week, but I admit I had been slacking. Ever since he told me he'd had a girlfriend since last summer, I decided it was for the best if I backed off. It'd be too messy. We used to make out in the library sometimes when I had a few hours' break during classes. Sexting slipped into our routine between withdraws from feeling each other up since I was still a virgin and wouldn't give in to him yet. Then he brought up the tiny fact that he was seeing someone else and I hit the brakes.

I still pined for him. I knew it was bad but I couldn't help it. I participated in these conversations with him because I secretly liked dangling what he wanted from me in front of him without ever surrendering. I liked this control over him. I replied:

You don't have any Friday nite plans? I didn't want to be annoying by texting you all the time. But I'm okay. Nothing to worry bout. =P

His response was delayed.

I always worry it's my hobby. And no, no plans. I don't really do the party thing much, my girlfriend went home for the summer, and all of my friends are busy.

Of course he had to mention his goddamned girlfriend. I told him he should try to find some new friends or something.

Not too interested. Plus I have you. :)

How sweet. But don't you want guys you can hang out with and stuff? =P

Not really, guys don't look nearly as cute. :P

I hate to admit this made me blush. I knew Emerson was an asshole and was just trying to sweet talk me so I'd do whatever dirty deed he had in mind. Guys hardly ever commented on my physical attraction and any compliment sucked me in.

I settled deeper into the couch cushions in my empty apartment and continued to type back. *Haha. They do if you swing that way. :D Besides, guys can't handle so much estrogen all the time. They need their testosterone fix. =P*

Fine if you don't want me to talk to you. :/

Emerson always did that too. He would get mopey and threaten some sort of ultimatum to which I'd have to quickly assure him I wanted him around. He had confidence issues, too. He once admitted he just liked knowing I still wanted him since apparently no one ever wanted him.

Emerson please. I'm kidding. Of course I want you to talk to me.

I knew you wanted it. :)

As always.

If that's true we should hang out soon. ;D

"Hanging out" was his code for getting together to make out. When I agreed, he told me I'd have to be really comfortable with the idea of "doing stuff" with him. I knew what this "stuff" was. I might have been a virgin, but I knew exactly what he was referring to. Most of his desires revolved around me being topless and on my knees. I asked him what he wanted to do.

Ehh... I want to cum on/in your mouth...

It was one of his biggest fetishes. I didn't understand how so, since I assumed every guy wanted to do this to a girl. The conversation was way past dangerous. I told Emerson we shouldn't be talking like this if he had a girlfriend.

I told you I'm bad with relationships, I'm not too good with being faithful. Plus I knew you first. Don't let that stop you, please.

He knew me first? What kind of bullshit was that? As if knowing me first gave him some sort of license to cheat on his girlfriend with me? His logic was fucked up, but the worst part was I was actually considering giving in to him. I had a hard time saying no and was inclined to entertain his wishes since I was still stupidly attracted to him and wanted to please him, even though the fact he had a girlfriend made me hesitant.

I don't need you tearing apart a relationship just because you want me to suck your dick.

You aren't tearing it apart because she would never know. I'm really asking you to not let this stop it. I'm being honest with you by letting you know she even exists. I'm smart enough to know what I'm getting myself into and how to handle myself, and it's not just about you sucking my dick, you know that.

Wow. Horrible. I knew he only wanted me to go down on him because there was never anything left after we made out or finished sexting. We weren't really friends, didn't know each other or spend any time together watching movies or playing games or just chatting. All we had was an attraction towards each other and sexual activities.

I tried to buy time to think by telling him I was still a virgin and didn't know what to do in bed. I didn't want to be a sex toy, but there wasn't anything else for me to be for him.

We don't have to have sex, plus I can tell you what feels good and what doesn't. I wouldn't leave you in the dark. Plus you learn quick, as I saw... and you are really good at bluntly talking dirty. It made me hard when you said 'me to suck your dick.'

I knew Emerson was just telling me anything to calm my fears so I would go along with this. I was sad to admit it was working and found myself agreeing to the idea more and more.

My intention wasn't to give you a hard on but if you like it I won't apologize.

Psh, you like it too. You should stop giving me maybes and tell me you actually want it.

Did I want it, though? I told him I did and I was just nervous. My fingers were buzzing from the unremitting texting.

It's okay to be nervous, get comfortable talking about it first. You'll do fine. I'll show and tell you what to do, little hints that you can get the rest from.

I exhaled and asked him if he was clean.

Yes, I am. I understand your worry. And if you get to be practical, so do I. Do you masturbate?

What fucking practicality did that question entail? A habit of masturbating and being free from any STDs were not in the same category. I told him I did occasionally.

Good, even if not constantly it shows you can be kind of lusty, I really find that hot. But I'm hard, so I'm kinda of using your answer for mental imagery.

The conversation proceeded to get raunchier as Emerson told me he wanted to get off to my dirty texts.

I'm definitely thinking of you right now, how badly I want you to want my dick and want to suck every last drop from it. You are definitely very lusty in my mind right now, I want to make you just as wet as I am hard right now.

I played along and supplemented Emerson with erotic images of me touching myself, but the beauty of texting was you could lie. How would the other person ever know? Sure I was indulging him so far, but I wasn't going to touch myself. My mind was too engaged in trying to wrap itself around the idea that I was really going to do this and let Emerson cheat on his girlfriend with me, even virtually.

Mmm. I'm rubbing myself. It tickles. My cheeks are flushed and my body's warm. Heart racing. Fast breathing. Thinking bout you touching yourself.

I'm doing the same, rubbing along my dick imagining it's you. And damn it this would be easier if we could talk on the phone, I have to stop touching to text.

It would *not* be easier if I could talk on the phone. It would be so much more awkward. The idea of phone sex terrified me because I'd never done it before and didn't want to reveal my naiveté.

So finish touching and then text. :D

Make me finish. ;P

I assembled some sort of finale text along the lines of rubbing myself and breathing really hard, blah blah blah. My phone started to pulse in my hand like a sick heartbeat. It no longer felt like a hard plastic phone, but a throbbing organ. I looked down and saw a dismembered penis pulsating in my palms. A warm, white fluid burst from the tip and spewed all over my shirt. The floor, couch, my clothes and hands were sticky with cum. I jumped up to run to the bathroom and frantically scrubbed my hands. I never liked being sticky or dirty. I checked the mirror to make sure there was nothing in my hair or on my face.

I heard my phone's text chime go off in the living room and tore away from my reflection. I found my phone, back to its normal plastic self, sitting on the floor beneath the glass coffee table.

Hope you didn't get sprayed too bad.

I read Emerson's text and frowned. Looking at the couch and the floor, I knew it'd take a while to clean up. *Eh, nothing to worry about.*

He didn't text back. I knew I'd heard the last of him for now, until he'd want to get off again in two or three weeks' time. I sighed, placed my phone on the coffee table and headed towards the kitchen to get some rubber gloves, a sponge and fabric cleaner. I needed a boyfriend—a legitimate reason to say no to Emerson. It was the only solution for ending things with him because there was no way in hell I was gonna spend the rest of my days cleaning my living room to erase his cum.

TAX FREE WEEKEND FUCK FEST
DONALD GEORGE LOSEY

and then they killed themselves bc suicide is deep.

"I'm not happy unless I'm raping the English language and drunk."

Andy ignored this.

Adam had his moods and despite having a personality that read like a 4chan.org post backwards, Andy was convinced Adam was the love of his life.

#onsomejoyceshit, Andy said, and they both chuckled while their Thursday night tempura sizzled on their reproduction antique vintage woodstove, which matched their wood window hangings expertly.

"Do you want to drink wine out of the bottle and laugh at str8 ppl?" one of them asked.

"No, let's just have a simple night at home, eat our tempura, then giggle in bed while we cut our-selves with the glass shards that are the only remaining remnant of the glass dildo you foolishly bought for me last Easter."

They sat down to dinner, contemplating identity politics and the various ways in which it ruined their lives and shoehorned them into a target demographic they didn't ever really want to be a part of.

"What a silly purchase," one of them said.

"Yes," said the other, "let me tell you a story"

"Okay tell me a story."

" I night I was not drunk enough and walking to the store to get drunk enough and a car came coming down the road and I said, hey you punk bitch ass–run me down why don't you, punk ass bitch, bitch bringing a car to a fist fight. Then I jumped in front of what turned out to be a truck, and was rewarded beau-co $ha money for my trouble."

"That was a nice story but if you were to write it down people who read it would be disappointed by the ending bc they're too stupid to realize it's the journey not the destination

Adam thought that through for a while, then came up with a brilliantly half assed solution

THE NEXT EXIT
EMILY AUMAN

With a darkened road before them, the couple sat silently with only the low sound of talk-radio hosts distorted from speakers long ago ruined from the heavy bass played over happier times. Fingers lazily entwined over a dusty gear shift, until the thin brunette in the passenger's seat pulls her hand away deliberately. She crosses her arms as if she's cold, but that doesn't seem feasible in August. Not cold, just distant. She can feel thumping against her chest as she considers the words the keep buzzing around her head. She feels so alone despite the breathing body so close to her. The hum of crossing a long bridge seems to invade their faux-quiet, the silence is heavy with intent. His long, blonde eyelashes blink, slow and measured, as he can feel the tension rise from her muteness. She wants to say something, she might explode if she doesn't. He rubs his right eye, trying to rid himself from emotional and physical exhaustion. He can't tell if it's coming from all the driving or all the rejection he's been facing, but he is tired.

"After this last bridge," she thinks to herself. She sees the end approaching, too fast, too sudden, and her heart throbs harder, vibrating through her ears and into her head. The sign, welcoming them into the next county, sits on the land's end as the water ends. "The water ends and so do we."

The end of the bridge comes, they take the slight bump back onto land the car keeps surging forward. She breathes easy, everything is still okay and nothing is over. Her heart rate slows just enough that she can think a little and her saline-tainted vision clears. He seems oblivious to her. That's the problem. He can tell that her mind aches and her eyes weep, but he doesn't care. How could he? She's been so cruel and withdrawn. She feels guilt hit her chest lightly at first, like a paperweight. Then it spreads, it gets heavier with each thought, as she feels the end come closer again and her heartbeat becomes audible once more. His eyes, a crystallized caramel, have always been so kind. She closes her eyes, thinking of the blank stares she's been using to purposefully alienate him.

She sees a sign marking an exit a mile ahead.

He can't focus. He can't get through to her. She won't look at him, she won't acknowledge he is anything greater than just another person. It is as if they haven't spent the last ten years together. As if they didn't work through it together when he lost work, when she felt uninspired, when they...

He feels a jolt in his car's speed as he involuntarily jerks his foot off the accelerator.

When they lost Elise. His vision goes to the memory of his wife's curled up form, sobbing, as the doctor's took the cold, tiny body away. He remembers the way she laid in bed and he left her side, long after he believed her to be asleep, to hear a little whisper as he walked away:

"I'm sorry."

The exit was coming up close and she could feel her pulse from her muscles to her teeth to her fingertips. The dirt under her nails distracted her for a minute and she welcomed the opportunity to think of anything but her plans to end her tainted marriage. A quarter mile ahead sat a well-lit exit ramp. They can't go on like this forever. It has to end.

His memory takes him to the way the light of a fading sunset bounced off of her hips one night on the beach. She was so beautiful, she didn't look so broken then. He glances at her in his peripheral vision and sees her arms twisted together, her mouth forming a firm line. She seems to be trembling a little, like she's nervous about something. He knows the exit ahead has an all-hours coffee shop.

"Sweetie, you want to stop and grab a coffee?" She looks at me, bewildered. Her arms fall a little, still crossed but less tense.

"Yeah, I think that would be good," she stops trembling and takes a deep breath, "I'm not quite ready for this trip to end yet."

He hates coffee. He hates being on the road any amount of time. She loves coffee. She loves riding. She cracks the window next to her and feels the breeze on her hair. It doesn't have to end. She, without realizing it, reaches out and takes his hand as the quiet tick of the turn signal beats in the time of her calmed heart.

VANILLA TUNA
LISA MUIR

September

"So you can be the Monday/Tuesday person and I'll be the Wednesday/Thursday person."

"And Friday?

"I figured Fridays we'd be on our own ... a day to maybe slip out and run errands, make an appointment ... without putting out the other person. Of course the schedule could be changed any time, at our mutual agreement. We'll start October first."

"And we should always be punctual."

"Absolutely. I'll be at your house at 7:25 on the dot every morning, whether to pick you up because I'm driving or to jump into your car because you're driving."

"And in the winter I'll have the car running so you don't need to move from your warm car to my freezing car."

"That would be nice."

"You don't have a problem leaving your car in my driveway all day?"

"Do you live in a bad neighborhood?"

"No ..."

"Dicey neighbors to worry about?"

"No ..."

"Then I have no worries. Doors will be locked. I keep no valuables."

"Should we have penalties for, say, being late, making the other person wait?"

"We won't be late."

"Deal."

"Deal."

October

"Glad I'm on time this morning. I know this sounds weird but the clock in my shower shows it's six."

"Who has a clock in the shower?"

"It's connected to a mirror, but it's dropped off the wall so many times that the clock doesn't function properly anymore. It just says six."

"When did this start?"

"Last month."

"You mean like it's 7:27 A.M. here in the car, so all the time your clock reads six o'clock?"

"No, just the numeral six. Digital thing."

"A single number? No clock time? Clock time should show several numbers, like seven twenty-seven has three."

"Right, plus a colon in the digital world. But I've only got the numeral six. A single six."

"And no colon."

"Nope, I don't merit a colon."

"And what do you make of this?"

"I figure its import will reveal itself over time."

"In the shower?"

"In the shower."

"In the shower things are washed away, become new. At least six is a spiritually positive number."

"How's that?"

"Six is the human number. Man was created on the sixth day."

"Well, my man was asleep this morning. It would have been helpful to know the time in the shower. Keep me on track. I lay my clothes out every night, for instance. Got to be organized."

"So do I. I can't think straight in the morning. I can't do anything without coffee."

"I need milk."

"Is coffee okay in the car? Your car I mean."

"Sure, got these handy cup holder holes right here."

"I wouldn't want to create a mess … like pretzels aren't a good idea."

"Funny how people drink coffee in the car but not milk. And pretzels, they're out."

"And I can't work at night, on school work, I mean."

"Me either. Sometimes I'll bring a stack of grading home just for show, but I never do it."

"I do the same thing. I'll pick up something and stuff it in my bag, especially if Krandall is still in her office and watching. I figure it gives that eagle eye of hers something to fix on."

"King Krandall, she may sign my paycheck but she sucks the life out of me."

"Do you know she used to grade our lesson plans? That was before you arrived."

"*Grade* them?"

"Every week. I used to earn just a C, and I'm great in the classroom, very effective. I wanted to throttle her."

"Can't say I'm anymore fond of her myself. When I first got here I nearly quit on the spot because she told me how she could deny my health insurance based on my performance. I thought, *How the hell do you think you can do that legally, bitch?*, but I needed the job. In retaliation I took a sick day and went shopping the next week."

"True confessions time I guess."

"What is it people say after being in Vegas? What happens in Vegas stays in Vegas."

"So what happens in the car pool stays in the car pool."

"Deal."

"Deal."

November

"Tonight, rather today, it's our anniversary."

"Oh! How many years?"

"Twenty-five."

"Congratulations!"

"Well, congratulations is actually sort of a weird response."

"But twenty-five years ..."

"Wish me a *happy* anniversary instead. Congratulations sounds like we've finished some great effort."

"I never thought of it that way."

"And I don't want it to be over."

"That's lovely. How's the number in the shower?"

"Still stuck at six."

"If the number goes down to five, that's grace. If the clock elevates to the number seven, spiritual perfection."

"I can't imagine any perfection on my part ... grace either. Thanks for warming up the car this morning though."

"No problem."

December

"We're at the number four in the shower."

"From six to four. Four is positive. Maybe it's a Christmas gift. You've progressed."

"Maybe it's a countdown. I must be a slow learner. It took two months to turn to a new number on the clock and I've gone backwards."

"Spiritually, the number four means you're grounded."

"But I jumped a number. Seems I'm regressing. I skipped five, that grace thing, like I told you. At this rate I won't get anywhere for another two months. I don't even know why we're discussing this number business."

"The number four means creativity, but creativity in a terrestrial way. That's where the grounding comes."

"I don't feel creative. What's a negative number?"

"Eleven ... eleven denotes disorder."

"That's me, an eleven. Long ago I was hired on the eleventh of August and even longer ago I was born on the eleventh of October."

"Well I'm obviously getting somewhere. Krandall smiled at me yesterday. Told me I was doing a good job and actually touched my shoulder. I didn't even get a horrifying burn mark from the hell fire in her fingers. I checked once I got home. Figured I'd have to take advantage of that health insurance if she'd made a permanent mark."

January

"I want to make a tuna casserole for them, you know, because they'll be home late after the visitation and they'll have all those out-of-town family members to feed."

"But we won't be to your house until 5:30 tonight and we've got to meet at the funeral home at 6:15."

"I can do it."

"Okay. Seems tight to me."

"I'm the one in the kitchen. I'll judge the time. But listen, let me ask your opinion, cooking-wise, I mean. I don't have any cream of mushroom soup."

"But that's key! It's the smoothing agent. My mother always made tuna noodle casserole with cream of mushroom soup."

"So did mine, but I'm thinking of just using some broth."

"Yeah, maybe to start with, but you need the creaminess."

"I've got a soy ... a vanilla soy milk."

"*Vanilla* tuna?"

"Or, I think I may have some sour cream. How about if I stir sour cream into the broth?"

"That sounds pretty repulsive as well. They don't mix."

"Maybe they don't mix for you."

"They don't mix for anyone. I'd never eat it."

"I don't recall asking you to eat it. But, maybe I'll just go to the store tonight and make the stuff tomorrow."

"That would be better. You've got to work with compatible ingredients."

February

"Geez, *pleeease* remember to warm the car in the morning."

"Sorry. Doesn't feel so cold to me."

"Well, it is. And the shower clock jumped to two."

"No three?"

"No three."

"Maybe this erratic jumping, it's trying to tell you something."

"No, you tell me what it's telling me. You're the numberology person."

"*Nu*-merology."

"Same thing."

"Not really."

"So tell me."

"I can't remember."

"Yes you can. Go ahead. You don't want to tell me, do you?"

"Three means completeness. That's what you've skipped."

"Completeness ... Is that a word? And are you implying I'm missing fulfillment in my life? I'm the one who's married, remember?"

"Two means difference. The world's off kilter. Something's missing."

"I'll say. And what if the clock turns to zero?"

"Zero doesn't exist on a clock."

"But what if it did?"

"Zero is a vanishing. It's so elusive that no one even knows who invented the concept of zero, though there are many theories."

"Spare me."

"It's just an empty place, a place holder. It's completely without value."

March

"Okay, I'm trying to understand. How come she asked you to chair this outside committee and not me? And who forgot to warm up the car again?"

"We'd spoken about it a couple of weeks ago."

"Without me?"

"I don't need to involve you in everything I do on school grounds. I'm my own person."

"But what about the car pool?"

"What about the car pool? The car pool is the car pool and school ... our positions ... are separate things."

"And I'll bet you've earned a raise for this."

"Yes, a small one."

"But we could have done it together."

"Could we? I'm beginning to doubt that."

"And we could have shared the small raise."

"Is that all you're thinking about? It's simply not in my purview to give you my hard-earned money."

"I see. A lot like it's not in my gastronomic purview to be eating vanilla tuna."

"Can't you let anything go? I didn't make it with vanilla, and I didn't make it for you anyway. Based on your recommendation, *your* recommendation because I listen to people and consider their opinions, I made regular old tuna casserole with the three main ingredients: elbow noodles, tuna chunks, and the goddamn *CREAM* of mushroom soup. The three heavenly ingredients, three, the number meaning completeness, if you remember, the word you didn't like. And the family really liked it. And they told me so. And I got a lot of satisfaction, which I'm not feeling at the moment sitting here."

"Completeness still isn't a word."

April

"You've got to stop slamming on the brakes for the butterflies."

"But I don't want them to land in the grill. I can't kill them, all that beauty."

"They're just butterflies."

"*Just* butterflies?"

"Plus, think scientifically ... or maybe mathematically ... you can't judge the speed and velocity of the common yellow butterfly as compared to the half-ton road vehicle."

"Maybe I could if I drove like you, always speeding. Hmm, how might one judge the velocity of the potential police car behind us ... ."

"I don't speed. I keep it to eight miles over the speed limit. No one is going to stop me for that."

"Okay, you use that logic when the time comes."

"Speeding, *official* speeding, starts at ten miles over the speed limit."

"Right, who told you that?"

"Let's keep in mind I've never *had* to use that logic because we've *never been stopped* when I've been driving. And if I remember right, the other person in this car *was* stopped not long ago."

"That wasn't for speeding."

"Still broke the law, not moving into the left-hand lane when the cop had that car stopped on the right-hand shoulder."

"But it was dismissed. Even the state admitted they'd just put that law into effect without any citizens' warning."

"Still sent you to court, sweet pea."

"This is a ridiculous conversation."

May

"How's the clock?"

"Stuck at two."

"Two is—"

"Don't remind me."

June

"You just hit the brakes to avoid that bird."

"No I didn't."

"Yes, you did. And you give me grief about slowing for the butterflies."

"*Slowing?*" You slam on the brakes and I'm not ready. Do you know what it's like not to be in control when you do that? Think about me in the passenger seat."

"That's what happens when you're a control *freak*."

"At least my vehicle is clean."

"And mine isn't?"

"You might clean it up Sunday evenings before we drive for the week."

"I can't help it if I haul around donated articles for Gently Used To You. You should try doing a good turn for others sometime. Are you even involved in a charity?"

"I write my checks ... plus, must be a bunch of junk you're hauling around if it leaves such a mess in the car. And why do you have to use my seat for that debris?"

"*Your* seat? This is *my* car."

"Yes, but you make the space available to me, as I do for you in my *clean* vehicle."

July

"I'm afraid, spiritually, I need to return to the numeral one."

"What's that supposed to mean?"

"… The committee is becoming too labor intensive."

"Is this the excuse you've come up with?"

"The number one, spiritually it means unity and commencement. It's time for me to move on, to start anew."

"So, we're finally at zero, place holders without value."

"You might check your clock."

"Your car is too cold anyway."

WE END UP HERE
CHLOE JOHNSON

Buckled in and safe from harm, Kathy and her daughter Olivia bounced—as much as their grayish seat belts allowed. Memorial Boulevard was bumpy. Kathy's eyes traced the tarred over cracks in the Rhode Island pavement.

"I want to be a taxi driver," Olivia said from the backseat. "With red hair." Kathy—who had blonde hair—watched her small, mousy brown-locked daughter fiddle with her chubby thumbs in the rearview mirror. Kathy didn't say anything, but sped up a little and sharply clicked her tongue against the roof of her mouth. It sounded like wooden clogs on concrete. Kathy was conditioned to be a svelte and polished housewife. Her mother taught her to place perfume at the back of her knees. Her father had equipped her with mace and spoon-fed her sunshine.

For the majority of her childhood, Kathy and her father had traipsed down to the coast along Memorial Boulevard and searched for seashells. Her father had created a contest to find the largest sand dollar. He rewarded her with a new pearl for her tennis bracelet. Kathy ran home with a small velvet box in her pocket every weekend. On their way home, they had counted the individual bricks on the Memorial Boulevard hand-laid barrier. Kathy made sure they counted in threes because the number comforted her. They strolled arm-in-arm and breathed in the salty wind. Near the end of their ritual walk, they ended up at a massive oak tree. They had counted the branches that extended toward the sky, lying on their backs, their legs outstretched.

Years later, Kathy often visited the oak to run her palm along the bark grooves, counting each ridge in a triplet rhythm. Most days she took the Memorial Boulevard loop. The loop consisted of driving along the beach for six miles, a left at Pennsylvania Avenue, and two more lefts after that to meet up with Memorial once more. She took this route exactly three times so she could glimpse the tree each time from her Range Rover.

In the summer before ninth grade, her father had lost a major client. At the same moment Kathy had pulled on crisp, dark jeans for her first day of school, her father catapulted a paperweight across his office. The heavy prism barely missed his boss' right earlobe. The family relocated to a neighborhood that smelled of tortillas and sewage. Kathy shared a room with her younger sister who always had frosting on her face. Kathy's mother purchased a sewing kit to mend old sweaters. Kathy was no longer able to put a Shirley Temple on the country club tab. She and her father visited the coast less frequently. The times they did, however, the sand dollars were her only reward. Her father had started selling cars. He spent his nights watching the stock market rise and fall, ushering in Kathy's dingy, pearl-less days.

She had counted the minutes and seconds until it was time to gather her neatly packaged crates and head off to college. She had dreaded another day spent watching her father's wrinkles deepen. She hated the way their conversations consisted of tuition costs and remember whens. Her diary was filled with angsty scribblings like, *He made a slow disaster out of me, out of all of us.* Kathy took tally of her pearl collection. It was all she had left of the father she used to gallivant with along the coast.

After graduating from a cheap, directional state university, Kathy had met her husband, Tom. She had found him brooding over a glass of scotch in a hotel lobby. He was travel-weary and his pockets were full of advertising executive-level cash. She had imagined Tom teaching her how to pronounce *foie gras* while rubbing her down with St. Tropez bronzing lotion in the Mediterranean. With a few calculated bats of her lashes and a seductive crossing of her legs, Kathy thought she'd be immersed in hot yoga memberships, strings of freshwater pearls, and a closet full of Manolo Blahniks.

Fast forward five years and he still hadn't taken her to Nice. He wanted to travel to places like Vietnam or fucking Scotland. He was hell-bent on expressing his love without the aid of diamonds and platinum. He forced her to watch BBC News. He placed literary *classics*, filled with his own margin notes, on her nightstand. Kathy let the books pile into stacks of three and after awhile, like clockwork, Tom patiently removed them from the table.

Kathy looked at Olivia's face in the rearview mirror. Olivia caught Kathy's eyes, smiled and said, "Daddy says I'm effervescent." Tom constantly patronized Kathy with big words, only now he was using their daughter as a megaphone. The small girl thought the world of Tom, mostly because he played into Olivia's God-awful idea of being a taxi driver for a living. *Taxi driving will get her nothing but poor, dirty men.* Kathy thought her daughter was stagnant. Olivia couldn't decipher between real and faux fur, had no idea who Prince Charming was, and certainly never had a silver spoon stuck in her mouth. Kathy and the brat were on their way to dance practice at Madame Edith's Ballet Company. *Click. Click. Click.* Forty-two miles per hour.

Tom had taken Olivia to the beach the previous week. He had told Kathy afterward, "We had such a fantastic time, Kathy. She and I wandered all over the coast." Kathy's face felt numb as she raced up the stairs. Sprinting into the girl's room she found a sand dollar the size of Saturn sitting on her shelf.

Kathy gripped the steering wheel tightly, wrapping her thumbs around the circumference. Olivia was looking out the right hand window. She pulled at the straps of her hot-pink car seat. "Mommy, can we go to the beach?" Kathy clicked her tongue and tallied the seams in the tar as they drove over them. She hoped to Jesus she hadn't left her curling iron on. She imagined Tom walking toward his car, carrying his keys, travel mug, and cognac-hued briefcase. He probably listened to shitty, whiny Derek & The Dominos on his drive home. *Just because his idiot of a son fell out a window doesn't make him a fucking musical genius.* She imagined Tom's veined hand gripping the luxuriously-stitched shifter as he maneuvered his way past traffic, absentmindedly mouthing, "Do you want to see me crawl across the floor to you." *Click. Click. Click.* Fifty-six miles per hour.

Kathy grew to hate Tom's obnoxious, orchestrated sleep-snoring. She often slept soundly in the guest bedroom, which afforded Tom the ability to sneak out in the wee hours. Kathy hired a private investigator to tail him, figuring she'd use Tom's money to pay for it once her suspicions were confirmed. His every moved had been recorded in a tiny notepad that sat in the P.I.'s pocket amongst stray coins and a pack of Parliament Lights. Pictures had been taken of him walking into his office building every morning. His receipts were recovered from Starbucks. Always one Venti Americano for $3.25, sometimes accompanied by a blueberry muffin. Last Tuesday afternoon, Tom had been recorded saying, "Have a nice evening!" to his co-worker as he opened his car door and slid into the camel leather interior. He then drove five miles to Marsden Elementary where he waited until Olivia burst through the glass doors.

Kathy wasn't satisfied with the P.I.'s findings. She believed he pocketed a majority of Tom's evidence for himself, stroking his thin mustache as he worked on a creepily rhinestoned Tom-dedicated scrapbook. The P.I.'s hands were always a bit sticky and she smelled rubber cement whenever they met. Kathy had googled the P.I. She had typed "Gregory Bradford" into the search bar. She noticed his name had only two 'o's. *Two was never a good sign.* His moniker had spelled out one thing to Kathy: Goddamned adultery. She was updated four times and—by way of pure female intuition—had drawn the conclusion that the P.I. and Tom were in cahoots, getting each other off while listening to Kenny Chesney.

Olivia made eye contact with Kathy in the rearview mirror. "Mommy! Unbuckle me, Daddy says taxi passengers don't have to wear seat belts." Kathy clicked her tongue again. *Fine. Twiddle your gorilla thumbs. You want to be a fucking cab passenger?* Kathy forced the car along faster.

She spun her head around and said, "If you want to ride in the taxi, Ma'am, it'll cost you." A droplet of sweat beaded at her widow's peak as she struggled to unbuckle Olivia's seatbelt. Her neck cramped as she finagled her arm around. She sped down the broken highway, gunning for a bump to bounce them again and send a shiver down Olivia's spine. They left an hour early to do the usual thrice round-about on Memorial Boulevard. Kathy turned her head to watch the salty waves roll in and veered onto the right shoulder a bit, unintentionally. An ambulance sped down the street past them, barely missing Kathy's left mirror. Olivia watched the lights fly by and said, "Mommy, what does that mean?"

Kathy responded, "It means someone got hurt." A huge back-up in traffic and an early left turn forced Kathy to interrupt the third round on Memorial Boulevard. Dampness accumulated at the back of her neck. She made her way back onto the familiar road again. *Click. Click. Click.* Sixty-five miles per hour.

Four miles down Memorial Boulevard sat the massive oak. It was spindly and bare in the cold damp of mid-March. Kathy balanced her forearms on the top of the steering wheel and gaped at the looming tree. *It never got old.* Suddenly, Kathy thought she saw hundreds of sand dollars hanging from the branches. She counted them all, mentally arranging them in triplets. The speedometer read seventy-three. Kathy was arrested by a vision of her father standing in the middle of the road. She leaned toward the windshield to watch as he tipped his Panama hat in her direction and smiled brightly. She slammed on her brakes with both feet to save him, to save what wasn't there. The Range Rover's tires screeched. A cool breeze brushed across Kathy's earlobe and cheekbone as her tiny passenger flew head-first through the windshield.

Kathy killed the engine and exhaled deeply. Her car was inverted and crunched by the steel guardrail. She squinted, examining the enormous oak through the shattered windshield. The massive tree trunk was painted in a trio of dripping red blotches where Olivia's head, shoulder, and leg had smashed against it. Blood dripped down to the base toward the tiny, broken body. Dappled sunlight danced upon Olivia's bloodied skin, making her sparkle. Kathy sat rigidly in her seat. Her hands clenched the steering wheel tightly until her knuckles were void of color. She clicked her tongue incessantly in threes until she began to hiccup, upsetting the rhythm. *Tom was right*, Kathy thought as she hiccupped again. Olivia was effervescent. She could see that so clearly now

ROAD RASH
BRIAN CULP

If he had told her once, he had told her a thousand times. Do not take the pump. Do not remove the goddamn bike pump from the garage. Please, honey. Pump your tires in the morning before you go. If the bike pump is in your car, then only one of us gets to use it. But if you pump the tires in the fucking garage, like I've asked on at least fourteen different occasions, we can both have properly inflated tires. Is that so hard? Is it too much trouble for you to think of someone other than yourself for a change? OK, honey? I mean let's not even discuss the fact that it's not safe to ride around on deflated tires. I mean, say I get a pinch flat out there and I'm stuck without an extra tube. I'm just gonna have to call you to come get me and then we both don't get to ride. See how that works? It affects both of us when you do something selfish like just throwing the pump in your trunk.

The man listened to his wife on the other end of the conversation for a moment before interrupting.

Look, whatever. I just don't want to have to tell you this again in two days, OK? Leave the pump in the god damned garage. All right? That's it, I'll see you tonight.

The man stabbed at the little red phone button on his phone, ending the call while she was still trying to get a word in. He then chucked the thing through the open window of his car. It bounced off the driver's seat before nestling into the well-conditioned leather upholstery of the passenger's side. If he wasn't in such a rush, he'd reach back through the window, grab the phone, and set himself a reminder: buy a spare pump. Just buy two pumps and keep one in the trunk, just so this kind of thing would never happen again.

In fact, he thought briefly about going inside and saying never-you-mind to the whole idea of going out for a ride that evening. But he was already dressed in his matching spandex kit, his water bottles were already full, and his helmet and clip-on shoes with the graphite footbeds were loaded in the car. He'd been really, really looking forward to the ride. The weather was perfect. Two of his best friends would be there. And he always got a much better workout in the big group rides—40 or more riders pushing each other ever faster, resembling a multicolored bait ball of ocean fish escaping a predator—rather than just going out by himself. So under his breath he muttered, fuck it, and threw the carbon-fiber bike with the under-inflated tires atop the four-hundred-dollar rack strapped to the back of his newly-waxed sedan, and headed out for an evening spin, if for no other reason than to give the circumstances of the evening the old middle finger. He was a hard-charging man who got what he wanted out of life as evidenced by his stainless steel appliances, his basement entertainment system and his wife's perfect breasts, all bought and paid for thank you very much. He wasn't about to be stopped by a few pounds of missing tire pressure.

The delay searching for the bike pump and then calling his wife almost made the man late, but he managed to catch a few green lights on the way, and pulled up just in time. One of his friends smiled and looked at his watch as the man unloaded the bike up and over the tines of the rack. The man was still adjusting his helmet when he said to his friend, "Wife took the pump. Don't ask."

"Wanna borrow mine?"

"No time," replied the man.

The friend shook his head and said: "Dogs and wives, my man. They're great to have around. Most of the time."

The man exhaled through pinched lips to acknowledge the jest. The sound was similar to the sound of air escaping a tire. He tucked his phone into the back-pocket pouch of his jersey and clipped shoe to pedal.

And then: about fifteen minutes into the ride, after the ol' thighs had gotten a chance to properly warm up, the man could already sense what toll the under-inflated tires would extract. It felt like he was biking over sticky pavement; it would take all he had to keep up with his friends, never mind the rest of the group. God damnit, the man thought. Wait 'till I get home. Just wait 'till I get home.

That was what he was thinking as he leaned hard into a turn. He was a hard-charging man, after all, and wasn't about to let other riders pass just because there's a little bend in the road.

He was doing about 25 mph at the time.

And because he was focused on the rider directly in front of him, and the pocket of wind resistance relief this position afforded, rather than on the road ahead, he didn't see the little sliver of a pothole—just a crack in the ground that had widened over the winter—and rolled right over the thing, same as the rider in front of him. Except that his under-inflated tube inside the bike's rear tire puckered up and over the bead of the aircraft aluminum wheel. There was a sharp crack from somewhere under his ass, he'd suffered a pinch flat, just as predicted. The man felt a needle of anger towards his wife course from his balls to brainstem, and he couldn't wait to make the call, the one where he could really let her have it, the one which would start with the question: "What did I fucking say about the pump, huh?"

But then the man wobbled. His back tire quivered like the hands of an alcoholic reaching for the afternoon's first drink. He tried his best to steer out of the surging bicycle paceline. In his anger, he overcorrected, jerking the handlebars rather than holding them steady and steering with the lean of his torso.

That's when everything went all to hell.

When he fell, the man's right forearm painted the middle of the street with a streak of bright, arterial red.

The car coming in the other lane didn't have a chance.

The driver would later explain, it all happened so suddenly. He had no chance to react. He was just going on instinct. There was a flash of movement, he said, his voice hoarse and detached, he did what he could. He had no possible way of knowing that locking his brakes would only make things worse.

The man, now on the pavement rather than on his bike, slid a few feet towards the oncoming car, and tried to put his arms up in a futile attempt to protect himself. The other bikers heard the scream of tires—a sound made by tires much thicker than those on a bicycle. And then the other bikers heard a low, sickening clunk that sounded like something large and hollow giving way; the sound the universe makes when it's being ripped apart.

The man under the car felt a blinding spike of pain, but where the pain came from didn't really register. And then, just as suddenly, the blinding pain was gone.

The man turned his head, although perhaps it was just his eyes. He saw another streak on the pavement painted with a multitude of hues: some bright reds, some darker, more muted maroons, and god knows what other colors mixed in. And then he saw his phone, resting on the pavement just beyond the streak. The phone. I need to get to my phone, he thought. I need to get to my phone to tell her what happened. I need to call her and describe all the colors I can see in this streak of red. I want to share the joy I feel beholding all this color, and I want to share it with her more than anyone else in this world. If I can just get to my phone, everything will be okay.

The man then tried to pick himself up, but his body would not obey the command. So he rested a moment, watching as his friends jog over to where he lay. Some other cyclists joined his friends. Their shoes were red and white and shiny, and they sounded funny, clip-clopping across the hard pavement like tap shoes across a stage.

"Holy fuck," one of the cyclists said when he arrived. His spandex was orange and white. "Holy fuck," another said, and then added: "God damn motherfucker." Another made a face and just turned away, placing his hands atop his head. This one's spandex bore a design with blue and red flowers. None of these riders were his friends.

His friends pushed past these other riders who were cursing too much, the man thought, and took up positions closest to him. One was tucking away his own cell phone; it looked like he had just finished a call. I wonder if my friend called his wife, the man thought. I wonder if he called and told her to come see the beautiful color painted on the street.

Both friends squatted down and slowly removed their helmets. What? What is it? the man lying on the ground asked. Is it bad? But the man did not hear the words escape his lips.

One of the man's friends—the one who had cracked wise about dogs and wives—put his hand on the man's ankle and left it there. The hand was warmth and comfort and hope. "Just stay down, buddy. Just take it easy. It's okay, he said in a soothing voice. It's okay. We're here. Someone's on the way."

The man's eyes shifted, and he saw the other friend. The other friend was not looking back, but rather at the one saying the soothing words. The other friend's eyes were big and shiny with tears.

I want you to grab my phone over there, the man said. Tell my wife I'm not mad. Tell her it wasn't her fault. Tell her I love her and I didn't mean it, any of it, the man said. But once again the words failed to form in his mouth. And then he saw why. Somewhere in the streak he painted on the asphalt, near his phone, was a purple lump, and the man now realized the purple lump was his tongue.

The man used all his strength and reached for his tongue. If only he could get the tongue back, he could use it to form the right words. He could use it to fill his mouth and his wife's ears with words that were kind and sustaining. He could tell his wife the things he had meant to tell her; the things he was *going* to tell her when he found the right time. He could tell her when she made bacon and eggs, it was the best meal in the history of the planet. That the time she helped him shave was the sexiest damn thing he can remember. That the best days of his life were the mornings they slept late on Saturdays, doing nothing other than listening to each other breathe. This was going to be easy, in fact: once he had his phone and his tongue back, everything would be okay.

He scrambled to his feet in order to regain his tongue, but for some reason only his hand seemed willing to carry out his mind's urging. "Easy, his friend said. Easy buddy. Just lie still. We're here. We're here." The man's other friend stared down at the pavement, clear drops of liquid splashing between those funny shoes that made the funny clip-clopping noises.

And so the man gave up the effort. All the color of the man's world slowly drained, and the purple lump he was staring at became gray, then black, and then the man stopped thinking about which words he might say, or how much air was in his tires, or tomorrow's budget meeting at work, or holding his wife close, inhaling the wonderful mystery of her as she rested on his chest, or whether it was safe to ride, or anything else. Every thought he ever had was now spilled onto the pavement, mingling with the two bright streaks of red he had painted a few moments ago.

DEATHWISH ON ACID
JEFFREY SYKES

He found risk inherent in certain forms, be it family, security or love. The specificity of risk excited Kyle. He could see the shockwaves pushing out from the epicenter of decision. The anticipation of reaction was his motivation. Imagine the problems this could cause!

He hadn't set out on this night to imbibe frenzy, but less than two hours after he'd downed the Death Wish on Acid he found himself neck deep in rivers of chaos.

The drive to Asheville had been tame, which was lucky on a Friday evening. His shift at the warehouse passed quickly given the amount of anticipation he had for the weekend at hand. His friend Norah had invited him to drive to see her brother. Kyle knew her brother, but was more interested in what might occur on the drive there and back. He had a sweet spot for Norah, one that longed to be assuaged.

He was able to score two grams of coke within ninety minutes of clocking out and was in Norah's driveway by a quarter past seven. The drive from Greensboro was mellow until they hit Morganton, the anticipation grew and they began to pull lines every ten minutes during the last hour of the trip.

Somewhere in McDowell County he pulled the Celica off the interstate hoping to buy a tallboy. The clerk gave him a funny look while mouthing the words "dry county" and Kyle had to content himself with Sprite.

The dry sweetness did little for his thirst, pushing him to drive carelessly up the serpentine concrete until they crested Black Mountain and floated along toward the I-240 exit that led downtown. Norah's brother, Troy, and his roommate, Kevin, gave them shit in a roundabout way for being fucked up, but they didn't push the issue. Troy had moved to the mountains to grow hydroponic pot, after all, and to escape the powder scene that dominated the mid-section of North Carolina at that time.

"Man, you guys are wired," Kevin said after they'd exchanged greetings and had the time to find a seat.

"Nah, bruh, just tweaked from the drive," Kyle said. "I tried to get us here as fast as possible."

Troy wasn't saying anything, just glaring at them because he'd specifically banned anyone from bringing blow into his house. Kyle tried not to look at him.

"So what's up with you two bitches anyway?" Norah said. "Are we going to hit the town or sit here and stare at each other?"

"We've been waiting on you, but now that you've arrived in style we can get the evening started," Troy said. "I guess you'll be wanting to smoke a bit so you can come down from 'the drive.'" He made quotation marks in the air before pulling a wooden tray from behind the apron around the bottom of the couch. A gray green glass pipe rested on its side surrounded by clumps of pot the size of grape clusters loosened from the bunch. Norah's eyes lit up and she licked her lips. "Yummy," she said and rubbed her hands together.

Troy pinched off a bit and stuffed the glass as Kevin got up and walked to his room just off the main living area. He opened and shut the door quickly, but not before Kyle saw the orange glow from the grow lights. "How's all that coming?" Kyle said, nodding his head toward the back.

"If by 'all that' you mean the grow room, then you know we don't talk about it," Troy said dryly. "But I can tell you that you'll enjoy this right here." He handed Kyle the glass and put the tray back under the couch.

Kyle's head still pulsed fifteen minutes later when Troy pulled his Civic under the I-240 bridge at Lexington Street. It was a good spot, just down the hill from Walnut Street. The lights from the storefronts and the rush of the crowd on either side gave him that electric Asheville vibe right off the bat. Straight-laced clean cuts in button down madras with badly dyed blondes in Eddie Bauer passed along amid dirty jeaned burnouts with unwashed dreads and ear lobes as hollow as their gaunt stare. Underfed women in formless cotton dresses tie-dyed the color of New Mexican sunrise tagged along behind hallucinating heroes tripping on the mellifluous din of a city open to possibility.

They crossed the street near Stella Blue and Kyle was almost knocked to the pavement by a gregarious high-class beauty dragging her high-heeled friend in a short skirt in the wake of her own flowing hair. Their toned forms backlit in the bluish streetlight as they ran toward the door. He thought to call out to them, and he would have in any other city, but he was trying to tap into that mellow Asheville soul.

He didn't want his reputation to follow him. Not here. Not when he and Norah had talked during the drive about moving up and joining the highland party. Not when he had the chance to leave his reputation for drunken brutality in the past and maybe find a way to tap into the good times vibe. If he could find a way to chill and leave the worries of the past in the past and not fret over them and chase the stoned just trying to mute the noise for a while.

"Where are we going, Troy?" he asked.

Troy had set a mighty pace and Kyle had fallen a few steps behind after he'd paused to watch the two dark-haired beauties rush into Stella Blue. He'd thought about running after them for a minute, but that's what got him into the trouble he was clawing his way out of eighteen months later. So he rushed to catch up to where Kevin and Norah walked arm in arm next to Troy.

"We're going to Magnolia's, behind that shop where you bought the ring last month," Troy said. "I met this cutie who tends bar there."

Kyle walked a few paces behind the group. He clenched his jaw and opened and closed his fists rapidly, trying to pass the pulse of envy he felt at the sight of Norah's arm fed through Kevin's, the way her hip and long torso brushed against his portly frame. Nothing he could do about it, he reminded himself. She'd made it clear to Kyle they wouldn't become lovers anytime soon. He'd cried on the phone a while back and said "I'll wait then" to which she replied "Don't" and he said "But that's all I have right now" to which she suggested they not hang out for a few days so he could get himself sorted out.

He'd fallen in love with her quickly after Troy left town and suggested Kyle hang out with Norah in his absence. He'd only been out of prison for six weeks when Troy told him he was moving to Asheville to get a new perspective.

Kyle didn't talk to her for a week after he'd finally said the words, but she'd called on Monday and asked if he wanted to drive up and see Troy for the weekend.

Magnolia's was a spacious bar with floor seating and dart boards on the wall and an opening that led to more restaurant seating and a billiard area next to bay windows. They shared a few drinks and caught up on small talk and Troy was able to make plans with his cutie. Norah walked off with Kevin to play pool and Troy finally turned his way.

"She's cute, huh," he said with a toothy grin as he turned to Kyle, who nursed perhaps his third Long Island.

"Very," he said. "But you always seem to make a good impression with them. I wish I knew how to do it."

"It just comes natural, bro, you just got to be yourself. I been telling you that for years now," Troy said. He smiled again with those easy eyes and then leaned back on his bar stool. "They're everywhere up here, man. You really should think about moving up," he continued. "And for real, you need to stay away from that shit in your nose. You're about to piss me off bringing that shit up here. And with my sister?"

"She's the one, homes," Kyle said quickly. "She's the one who calls me on the phone 'hey watcha doing? Wanna split a gram?' You know I'm struggling, and all alone, so what am I gonna say when a 21-year old asks me do I want to go out and get wasted?"

Troy looked at his beer. "I know. Look, you should know that my parents are suspicious. Asking me all kinds of questions about who she hangs out with and is she hooked on drugs, so try to get her to chill."

"I try man, but ever since she started tending bar at Stilskins shit is crazy."

"Yeah, my mom is about to come down on that, too."

"So, it's like half the time I am trying to protect her and half the time I am trying to do my thing. Did she tell you I almost got in a fight with a guy who wanted to hit on her about two weeks ago?"

"Yeah, I heard."

"I mean shit Troy, I can't be violating my probation. I got thirty-six months hanging over my head. It's one thing to do dope, but if I get arrested, I'm fucked."

They passed a few minutes in silence and Kyle turned around and leaned his elbows on the bar. He watched Norah from across the room. He'd fallen in love with her because she was Troy's sister and he missed Troy with all his heart. He knew this much. He knew what his feelings for Norah amounted to. And that's what kept him from running off the rails like he'd done so many times before.

"I miss you brother," Troy finally said to him. "I hope you can get this way. It would be good for you."

"I'd really like that," Kyle said. "Maybe things will line up and I can make it happen. Make a few good decisions for once." The comment lingered between them, hovering in the possible space before pushed away by the sound of Norah's voice from the other end of the bar.

"Kyle, get down here," she called, leaning her breasts upon the bar so that he could see her smile beyond the row of people between them. She was with Kevin and had picked up a couple more admirers, an athletic black man in a gray shirt stretched across his thick chest, and a tall blond school boy in khakis and a red and black polo shirt. Kevin knew them, they formed a tight circle around Norah. One had his hand on her hip near the space where her shirt rose up from her belt line to expose her taut midriff.

Norah was like her brother in that they both were wholly without malice and often the center of the party. But unlike Troy, she was still very naive. "Not this shit again," Kyle thought when he saw the dark-skinned hand resting on her hip. He approached gingerly, as if afraid of being drawn into another conflict over who earned her attention.

"Dude, you have to try this," Norah said. She handed him a tumbler, with colored liquors stacked in layers.

"What is it?" he said and raised the glass to his nostril.

"Death Wish on Acid," she said. "It is so good."

Kyle didn't think it sounded like a good trip. He sniffed the liquor, picking up hints of rum, whiskey and mint.

"Don't be a fucking pussy," Norah snapped. He downed the shot, surprised at how effortlessly the concoction went down.

"Let's do another," she said. Kevin and the two suitors nodded.

"Why not," Kyle said.

Norah stepped up onto the foot rail and leaned in to get the bartender's attention. The school boy elbowed his dark skinned friend, they eyeballed her ass and the school boy made a groping motion with his fingers. They both looked up to Kyle, the school boy offering a lecherous smile as he pulled on his cigarette and looked away through the rising smoke.

She handed around the drinks and they downed them without a word. Norah turned and accepted the touch of her suitor. Kyle looked back down the bar to where Troy laughed with a new group of friends. Kevin and the school boy chatted about a mutual friend from the restaurant where Kevin worked.

Kyle lit a cigarette and contemplated the visible. The energy, like atoms in constant vibration, giving, receiving, moving without reason. He realized he'd reached the point of inebriation that he called "liquefied" where the infusion of more alcohol leads only to nausea. He stood sipping a glass of water when Troy said he was ready to bolt.

Kyle rode in the backseat becoming increasingly disoriented. But he snapped to when Troy took a clover leaf curve too fast and came within four inches of the concrete barrier that separated them from the French Broad River flowing silently below in the darkness.

"It's all good!" Troy yelled as he worked the wheel, his hands crisscrossed as the tires screamed before he righted the small white car and they all laughed.

"Holy shit," Norah said. "I need a cigarette." She smoked for a minute and then asked Troy if he would stop at the grocery store.

"Will you run in for us, Kyle?" she said. Still buzzed from the hairpin curve, he thought it would be a good decision to get out of the car for a minute. Troy handed him ten dollars and said to get a couple of cheap pizzas and a Coke, and maybe a pastry for in the morning.

The store was incredibly bright, Kyle felt a strange rush of drunken energy, a manic, confused excitement, as if he was just getting his alcoholic's second wind. He did grab two pizzas and a Coke, and some Pop Tarts, and headed to the front. It dawned on him as he waited at the register, he hadn't seen anyone else in the store. Not a clerk. Not a customer. Not a cashier. He thought about laying the ten spot on the counter, but he looked around again, and seeing no one, he walked out the door.

The excitement bit into him. The electric tingle of fear as he waited to hear a voice calling him to stop, footsteps rushing in syncopated loss prevention.

He exited the foyer and went through the large sliding door. Down the concrete sidewalk and across the blacktop to the white car. He could see Troy laughing in conversation. He glanced back over into the store and still saw no one at the checkout. It was like an apparition of a grocery store, a third moment between what normally is.

INTERSTATE EXIT
JIM DOERING

They both stared up at the water-stained ceiling, lying side-by side on a lumpy queen bed at a rundown motel in a sketchy part of Kansas City. It was located near the interstate at the beginning of the bad part of town.

"Until this second, I hadn't noticed that big stain on the ceiling," he said. "It reminds me of two people, connected together."

"To me it looks like two kidneys bleeding out, blood pooling between them." She glanced at the cheap alarm clock on the nightstand. "We have to go soon."

"I know. I just wish we had more time. We always need more time." He glanced at his watch. It was the only thing either of them was wearing.

He turned to her, his head never lifting from the flat pillow. "How many times have we been in this motel, do you suppose?"

She didn't turn to meet his gaze. "How many years, is more like it."

Sighing, she wrapped the scruffy sheets around her petite form as she rose from the bed. She sat up, feet touching the floor, her naked back exposed to him. The bed sheet snaked around her waist. He scooted up, propping the pillow behind him against the dark-stained walnut headboard with cigarette burns on the top. The position made his middle-aged paunch more prominent.

"If you really want to talk about this we can stay a little longer," he said.

"No, you said it yourself. There's so little time." The bed sheets snaked around up to her shoulders. Her lips pulled tight, she said, "Don't you have a lot of work back at the office? I'd hate for you to be late for dinner." She inspected the floor near the cheap-looking oak-paneled walls.

"What are you looking for?" he asked.

"My underwear. It has to be down here somewhere."

"I didn't take them this time, I swear," he said. She looked back and rolled her eyes, lifting the burnt-orange bedcover, which had slid down and pooled on the stained, dull-green carpet.

"Here they are," she announced, snatching up a twisted wad of lacy black fabric. "They were hiding." She stood, letting the sheet slide from her torso, exposing her pert ass. She lifted a leg and pushed it through the leg hole of the panties. In a moment she had pulled on a matching bra. Turning to him she raised an eyebrow. He took the cue and jumped out of bed to the carefully folded stack of clothes sitting on the rattan-backed desk chair. In a few minutes they were both dressed, him in a charcoal grey suit and her in a bright-blue dress with black stilettos.

"Ready?" he asked as he tied a black wingtip with a tight double knot.

They marched to the battered exterior door covered with multiple coats of dull, dirty paint. He opened it wide. Bright light invaded the room as he turned and faced her, the sun glaring around him.

"Do we dare risk one last bit of affection with the door is open and the world able to see us? Or would that violate your rules about PDAs? He asked.

"Don't be silly," she said, holding out her arms. He went to her, hugging her tightly, but when he tried to kiss her, she turned her face away. Instead of soft, supple lips, his kiss landed on her cheek. Frowning, he continued, his thin lips lingering over her soft, rosy skin before he buried his nose in the side of her neck, inhaling deeply.

"I love the smell of you, woman." She gave a little laugh and pulled away.

"It's the smell of yourself you like. You've marked your territory." She launched herself through the doorway and into the light. The sun was high and a blast of heat assaulted them both as they hit the sidewalk. A car alarm went off on the other side of the deteriorated parking lot. Before she could step off the sidewalk and to her car, he grabbed her hand and yanking on her arm, pulled her back into the motel room, closing door behind them.

"What are you doing?" she demanded, not smiling. The brightness outside blinded them making the room darker. He pulled her past a chipped, round table near the door and sat her down in a chair with a cracked leg. He sat down on the edge of the messy bed, still holding her hands.

"When we play tennis after work and you look at me when we're done, the perspiration running down your neck, I want to hug you so our sweat mixes together. After we've made love, and I roll over, I breathe deeply near you because it's the smell of *us*. Not me, *us*." Embarrassed, she slid her hands from his. He grabbed them back so tightly she winced. He went down to the floor, chest against her knees and gazed into her eyes, forcing her to look down. "And when I told you I loved you but you said you didn't feel the same way, and hugged me close and said you were sorry, all I could think of was the smell of *you*. Even if you don't love me, your fragrance reminds that at least you're here. This is real life. It may not be perfect, it may not be everything, but it's something."

"I never meant to hurt you," she said, her voice distant. Barely above a whisper, she stroked the graying hair at his temples and said, "It must hurt a lot."

"I think about it all the time," he said. His dipped his head down to her lap and closed his eyes. They were still for awhile, her hand on his head. The sound of their breathing moved in tandem, keeping time against the noisy hum of the wall-mounted air conditioner.

Minutes passed. When he rose there was a wet spot on his tie. He picked her up and she let him. He placed her atop the still-damp tangle of sheets, her eyes wide. His already closed. He kissed her deeply, his hands holding her face so she couldn't turn away again. Their faces became hot and sticky from saliva and tears. He smiled through swollen lips. She pulled a tissue from somewhere in her dress and dabbed at her moist eyes.

"We need to get back to work." she said, her voice firm. She gently pushed him away, dropping the tissue as they rose from the bed. They quickly straightened their clothes and he opened the door once more. She left first, and he took one last look at the room before following.

The afternoon sun glared off the windows of the cars on the cracked lot. They went to the space between their two vehicles and faced each other.

"So, Thursday night tennis?" he asked. "We can have a bite after."

"There's something I need to say." She inhaled deeply, and when spoke it was as if she was out of breath. "I've been seeing someone," she said. "He's not anybody you know."

"Oh," he said, falling back against his car.

"We knew this day would come eventually. That I'd meet someone."

"Do you love him?" he croaked. She looked outward, into the distance and toward the interstate. The sun reflected intensely off her large, black sunglasses. She was silent. "I guess there's not much left to say."

"That's up to you, I suppose," she said. A heavy silence grew between them. Nodding to herself, she opened her car door, climbed in and started the engine. Her closed window between them a curtain, she looked ahead as her call eased forward.

He remained, unmoved. He watched her drive off the motel lot, disappearing up a ramp to the highway. Sweat was soaking through the collar of his starched white shirt as the fierce sun beat down upon him. He looked at his meticulously tied shoes, and squeezed the damp tissue, rescued from the bed and still wet from her tears. He slowly raised it to his face and breathed in. An endless stream of vehicles hurtled down the interstate, past the motel exit. Each moved their passengers to more important places.

ABOUT THE AUTHORS

Nikita Hernandez was born and raised as a military brat, or "professional gypsy" as her mom likes to say, Nikita Hernandez grew up in the Deep South drinking sweet tea and plucking pecans from her next door neighbor's tree. She spends her time daydreaming, doing arts & crafts/DIY projects, and drinking tea. This is her first fiction publication. Nikita dabbles mostly in poetry and has been nominated for the 2016 Pushcart Prize. Read more of her stuff at http://nikitahernandezpoet.tumblr.com/.

Larry Lefkowitz (born 1937) grew up in The U.S. and immigrated to Israel in 1972. He has previously published the literary novel "The Novel, Kunzman, The Novel!" and his anthology "Laughing into the Fourth Dimension, 25 Humorous Fantasy and Science Fiction Stories." He has had many short stories published in journals, anthologies, and online.

Brian Culp is an agented writer who has sold more than a million words of non-fiction, and is a 2014 alum of the Iowa Writers Workshop. He lives in Kansas City.

Chloe Johnson drinks espresso and craves gin, but usually not together. She studied Creative Writing at the University of St. Thomas and served as editor of the Summit Avenue Review. She gathers peculiar moments into tiny notebooks. Her stories explore the unsettling and painful layers of everyday people wrapped inside the mundane and familiar. She lives in Kansas City.

Richard Cabut's fiction and poetry has appeared in various magazines and books. His plays have been staged in fringe London theatres. He has also written for several national newspapers and media organizations. In the past, he played bass and proselytized on behalf of the punk group Brigandage. He lives in London, and works as a writer

Donald George Losey was born in North Carolina in 1988. His work has been published on www.old67.com as well as The Salmagundi: an Anthology.

Victoria Briggs lives in London and is a graduate of Middlesex University's Creative Writing MA. She has worked previously in magazine publishing and once won the Asham Award for women writers. She has had stories published in Quarterly Women's Fiction and Prole magazine.

Jeffrey Sykes has written poetry and songs since childhood. After working as a journalist he's begun to explore his dream of writing fiction. A student of history, he enjoys good writing in all forms. Follow him on Twitter @jeffreysykes

Emily Auman is in her early twenties, her greatest pastimes almost exclusively involve alcohol and poorly-written television shows from the early 90s. She resides in the foothills of North Carolina and firmly believes the term "foothills" is a weird one. Follow her musings at emilywrites.net.

Jeffrey Garver is a writer living in Burbank, California.

Lisa Muir has taught English for more than thirty years and strives to enlighten students about composition, literary research, and American Literature at Wilkes Community College in Wilkesboro, NC. She has published research in academic journals and hopes to find more time to pursue fiction publication.

Jim Doering's stories have been featured in *Meat For Tea*, *Punchnel's*, *Mad Scientist Journal*, *The Daily Palette*, *Prime Number Magazine*, *Blue Monday Review*, and the anthology *The Salmagundi*. His work has been nominated for the *Pushcart Prize*. He serves as Executive Editor of Blue Monday Review.

Victoria Briggs lives in London and is a graduate of Middlesex University's Creative Writing MA. She has worked previously in magazine publishing and once won the Asham Award for women writers. She has had stories published in Quarterly Women's Fiction and Prole magazine.

67 Press is a literary publishing collective founded to give fringe authors a vehicle to be heard. Our goal is finding talented people on the edge of society with something to say, but don't fit into a neat little box for mainstream publishers. We find talent and help that talent work within their vision to create a finished product. We do all the things that other publishers do, but we do it with the author in mind, not the bottom line or focus groups. We would never tell an author their book doesn't fit into a specific genre, it's too audacious or "we just don't think it will sell". We believe great stories and great writing transcend subject matter and audience.

If we sound like a publisher you want to work with, please contact us we'd love to hear from you:

http://67press.com/contact-67-press/